THE SIXTH
Demon
BOOK ONE

Other books by R. A. Steffan

Circle of Blood: Book One
Circle of Blood: Book Two
Circle of Blood: Book Three
Circle of Blood: Book Four
Circle of Blood: Book Five
Circle of Blood: Book Six

The Last Vampire: Book One
The Last Vampire: Book Two
The Last Vampire: Book Three
The Last Vampire: Book Four
The Last Vampire: Book Five
The Last Vampire: Book Six

Vampire Bound: Book One
Vampire Bound: Book Two
Vampire Bound: Book Three
Vampire Bound: Book Four

Forsaken Fae: Book One
Forsaken Fae: Book Two
Forsaken Fae: Book Three

The Complete Horse Mistress Collection
The Complete Lion Mistress Collection
The Complete Dragon Mistress Collection

Antidote: Love and War, Book 1
Antigen: Love and War, Book 2
Antibody: Love and War, Book 3
Anthelion: Love and War, Book 4
Antagonist: Love and War, Book 5

THE SIXTH

Demon

BOOK ONE

R. A. STEFFAN

The Sixth Demon: Book One

Copyright 2021 by OtherLove Publishing, LLC

All rights reserved. Printed in the United States of America. No part of this book may be used or reproduced in any manner whatsoever without written permission except in the case of brief quotations embedded in critical articles or reviews.

This book is a work of fiction. Names, characters, businesses, organizations, places, events and incidents either are the product of the author's imagination or are used fictitiously. Any resemblance to actual persons, living or dead, events, or locales is entirely coincidental.

ISBN: 978-1-955073-17-2 (paperback)

For information, contact the author at
http://www.rasteffan.com/contact/

Cover art by Deranged Doctor Design

First Edition: January 2022

Author's Note

This book contains adult material. It is intended for a mature audience.

Table of Contents

PROLOGUE

It took one hundred and eighty-three years to learn the guard's trust.

By then, she was fairly confident her demon captors had forgotten about her presence in their prison, at least for the most part. They'd been foolish to assume a Seelie Fae prisoner would be incapable of playing the long game, simply because she had stumbled into Hell with missing memories and no name to call her own, in the aftermath of the Great War.

Leyak, the imp who'd been assigned by the Demon Council to guard her, leaned casually against the iron bars that formed the front wall of her cell. "How is it that you, a Fae, can understand me better than anyone else in the three realms?" he asked.

Perhaps because you are a simpleton, and no one else cares to make the effort for fear of the crushing boredom that would result, she thought.

Fae couldn't lie, so aloud she only said, "You are not so difficult to understand. Is being understood for one's true self not a common desire?"

Leyak considered that for a moment. "I suppose it is," he agreed. "Nevertheless, are you absolutely certain you wish to go through with the soul-binding?"

In a way, this whole thing had almost been too easy. The Council had assigned her an imp guard, rather than a succubus or a demon of fate. It had probably been meant as a magnanimous gesture… an unasked for kindness, intended to honor the completion of the successful peace treaty with the Fae Court.

Imps were drawn to magic, and she had magic aplenty—hidden though it might be. It took time, but the poor fool would never have been able to resist her indefinitely.

"I'm certain," she said, batting wide, green eyes at him. "I feel confident that with the bond between us, I will finally be able to recall my name and why I came to be here in Hell. I don't wish to be trapped here forever, Leyak. Perhaps if I am able to give your Council the answers they seek, they will consider lenience."

"You miss your home," Leyak said, with clear compassion. "You miss the Fae realm of Dhuinne."

"I do," she agreed, and every word she spoke was the truth. "It's a good bargain, and I wish to strike it with you… only you. If we are successful in unlocking my memories and passing that information to your superiors, that success will advance your position among your people. It would also give me a chance at what I desire—returning home someday."

Hell was a prison that had nothing to do with this roomy, furnished cell carved into the living rock. Anyone could enter this barren realm, but only demons and those bound to them could leave. It was the only reason the demon stronghold had escaped direct attack during the war — any invading force would immediately become trapped here forever.

Leyak nodded, as though to himself. "Then the bargain is sealed." He lifted a small, faceted stone, like glowing quartz. "I've acquired a bonding crystal. Probably best not to ask how I got it."

"I would never presume such a thing," she said solemnly.

He nodded again, clearly nervous, and unlocked the cell door. He was careful to lock it again once he was inside, as though an iron lock would be enough to thwart her once she had what she wanted from him.

"You understand how this will work?" Leyak asked. "You'll be selling your soul to me. It can't be undone."

"I understand." She extended her hand, palm up.

Leyak took it gently in one of his and placed the crystal in it. With his free hand, he drew a dagger from his belt. Still cradling her hand holding the crystal, he drew the sharp edge against the base of her thumb. Blood welled up, staining the brilliant facets. He let her go and sliced his own palm open, moving to clasp her injured hand with the crystal pressed between them, so that their blood mingled.

She held his granite-colored eyes, unblinking.

"It is done," he said, releasing her and plucking the crystal from her grip. He crushed it in his fist with demonic strength, letting the tiny, red-stained fragments rain down to clink lightly against the stone floor. "Your soul is bound to me, nameless Seelie. None can tear asunder what magic has constrained."

"Oh, good," she said, her magic and her memories unfurling from where they had lain dormant for nearly two centuries, waiting for this moment. "It's about bloody time."

Leyak looked at her in confusion, only to gasp when her hand darted forward to clasp his cool forehead, her palm covering his invisible third eye. She let the magic rush through her and into him, focusing every ounce of strength she possessed on bending his will to hers.

The imp's mind struggled and thrashed against her. "What—" he gasped. "What *are* you?"

She smiled at him, baring sharp canines. "I suppose I did tell you that with the bond, I would be able to recall my identity and why I came to be here in Hell. I am Dhuinne's Midwife, Hellspawn. I renounced my name and my memories that I might come here in secret to learn your people's weaknesses. The Fae Court may be content to bargain and appease, now that the war is over—but I will not be content until Hell is destroyed utterly."

Leyak stared at her, wide-eyed. "No..." he murmured, right before his will succumbed to hers.

⊰◆⊱

It was a simple enough thing to pry memories from the imp's mind. She sought images of two high-ranking demons who would be able to pass through the gate linking Hell to Earth without being questioned. After glamouring herself and her former captor to resemble the pair, she compelled Leyak to unlock the cell and let her out. At her mental direction, he led her to the caves that housed the barrier separating Hell from Earth.

The guardians of the gate nodded respectfully as the pair entered, wearing their flawless magical disguises. In a daze, Leyak guided her to a section of rocky wall and ushered her through. Magic slid across her as she passed out of the demon realm, her body protected from the barrier by the soul-bond she'd allowed him to forge with her.

Utter darkness lay on the other side. She summoned a glowing ball of light and set it floating above her, illuminating a pile of tumbled boulders leading down to a natural underground tunnel. The eerie sound of wind moving through narrow passages brought to mind the wailing of doomed Fae being consumed by the Wild Hunt.

A shallow pit lay on the uphill side of the tunnel. The air coming from that direction held the faint scent of the distant surface. She led Leyak in the other direction, deeper into the underground cavern. When she reached the edge of a second, much larger pit, she clamped down on her control of the foolish imp's mind to keep him quiet.

The short sword he wore at his belt was not her preferred weapon, but in the absence of her beloved saber, it sufficed to hack off the idiot's head. Once it was free of his body, she wasted no time splitting his skull in two.

Demons were functionally immortal, but she only needed him insensible and helpless for a few hours. She threw one half of the head in the deep pit. Then she cut out his heart and stuffed it, still beating, inside her tunic to carry. She hauled the other half of his skull back to the shallower pit and tossed it in, confident that it would take him a while to magically recall all of his various pieces across that much distance.

After wiping the blade clean on her buckskin breeches, she tucked both his sword and the dagger he had used for the bonding ceremony into her belt. Casting a magical travel portal into existence, she stepped through the flaming oval to freedom.

She'd expected to find herself in the arid, nameless wilderness that surrounded the cavern containing Hell's hidden gate. Instead, she stepped into bright sunshine illuminating a garish, human-made structure. "*Moaning Cavern Adventure Park,*" proclaimed a sign in Earthen English. "*Twin Zip 1500 Feet Open Daily.*"

The message was cryptic and the surroundings strange, but it was clear enough that humans had encroached into the area and set up habitation. Several of the creatures were wandering around, and a few turned sharply to look at her after her sudden appearance. She sent out a wave of subtle power to quiet them. The humans' eyes grew dazed and uninterested as they returned to what-ever they'd been doing before her abrupt arrival.

Truly, the presence of this strange outpost was a blessing straight from Mother Dhuinne. She'd assumed she would need to find the closest native settlement on the banks of the nearby river—but there were humans right here, ripe for the taking.

What she had planned was distasteful in the extreme. It would also result in her death… at least, in a manner of speaking. Still, her sacrifice would be worthwhile if it made possible the ultimate destruction of the Fae's ancient enemies. She mounted the wooden steps leading up to the structure and entered it. The inside was an explosion of useless items—rocks and ugly clothing, books, boxes, and trinkets of all description. A young human female with dark hair and brown eyes stood behind a counter piled with more meaningless detritus.

The human's eyebrows went up. "Whoa," the creature said, in bastardized English. "That's some nice cosplay! Hey… wait. Are you all right? Is that blood on your shirt?"

She let her power unfold once more. The human's will bent to hers with only a fraction of the effort it had taken to overpower her demon guard.

"Take me somewhere private, where we will not be disturbed," she commanded.

The human's expression went abruptly blank. It stepped from behind the counter, and she followed it to a room near the back of the structure. The place stank like a latrine, the scent of bodily waste overpowered by an appalling chemical stench that made her nose burn. The creature closed the door behind them and engaged a metal locking mechanism with a click. Unnatural lights flickered into life above their heads, the sickly glow contained within long glass tubes.

Her lip curled with distaste, but she set aside the unpleasantness of her surroundings in favor of focusing on the next stage of her plan.

"Look at me, creature," she commanded, placing one hand over the human's heart and splaying the other over its forehead — much as she had done to Leyak. "I have need of your body."

A flare of primal fear ignited behind the human's eyes for the barest of instants before she reached inside and took control.

ONE

The murder victim had already been removed from the gift shop restroom by the time Neveah Lane arrived on the scene. That was no real surprise—while she kept a sharp eye out for odd occurrences around Vallecito, with the help of a police scanner app dialed in to the area, it was still a solid hour's drive to get here from her apartment in Stockton.

The Morning Watch website paid Neveah to write up interesting news content for them as a freelance reporter. While sticking her nose in where it wasn't wanted had been her primary occupation for a solid couple of millennia now, receiving money in return for her snooping was a relatively new phenomenon.

She hoisted her camera bag into a slightly more comfortable position and pulled a notebook out of her pocket. "So, you didn't see the victim come into the shop?" she asked the pale, acne-pocked teenager standing behind the sales counter as though it could act as a bulwark against the outside world.

He shook his head rapidly, pushing his black-rimmed glasses up his nose when they slipped. "No, no one did. It was really weird. Alice was watching the counter. I was outside getting the zip lines set up. But there was a pretty good-sized crowd wandering around—mostly outside, in the adventure park area."

Neveah dutifully jotted this down, giving him a brisk nod. "Right. But you were the one that found the body?"

Another frantic head shake. "No—I mean, not exactly. The body was the women's restroom. A customer found it and I came running when I heard the screaming. It was crazy, too. This beautiful woman—and I'm talking, like, supermodel gorgeous—dressed up like Tauriel from Lord of the Rings, with blood all down her front."

Neveah raised an eyebrow, but covered the reaction quickly. "Do you know what killed her? Did the police say?"

"I don't think they know for sure yet," said the teenager. "Shot or stabbed, I guess, with all the blood. I'll tell you what was the weirdest part, though. She looked... *peaceful*. Her eyes were open, staring up at the ceiling. But she had this strange little smile on her face. Like—er, what do they call it? A Mona Lisa smile. That's it. Just like in the painting."

"Hmm," Neveah replied absently, already planning her next steps. "That's interesting. Thank you so much for your help. One more thing—you mentioned a coworker who was inside the gift shop when the dead woman arrived. Alice?"

Worry clouded the kid's face. "Alice Ramirez, yeah. She, uh... she disappeared. I think maybe she saw what happened in the bathroom and got upset. And then she, like, ran away, maybe? The police seemed really interested in talking to her, but no one knows where she is right now."

Neveah didn't doubt that the police were interested. She jotted the name down, and wrote '*Suspect*?' next to it. "I see. I don't suppose you know where Alice lives?"

"No, only that she's got an apartment in Vallecito. She's a college student at Columbia. I guess her parents are loaded, but they wanted her to work during the summers for the experience." He fumbled behind the counter and came up with a cracked wooden clipboard. "Hang on, I've got her cell number here. I already gave it to the police. And I tried to call her earlier, too, but it just went to voicemail."

After taking down the phone number, Neveah thanked him again and went to scope out the restroom in question. Unsurprisingly, the area around it was surrounded by crime scene tape and guarded by a stoic female police officer. The woman lifted a hand in warning as Neveah approached.

"No press allowed past the yellow tape," the officer said. "This is an active crime scene; you'll need to stay back."

Neveah smiled at her, watching as the woman blinked rapidly in response, her lips parting slightly.

"I understand," Neveah told her, letting her aura unfurl from its usual tight restraints. "And I really do hate to ask, but it would mean *so* much to me if you could let me have a little peek inside. It'll just be for a moment, promise. I'll wear the cute plastic booties and everything."

The officer's expression grew dazed, adoration shining in her eyes. "J-just for a minute, right?"

Neveah turned her most dazzling smile on the woman. "That's right, dear—I just need a *teensy* peek. No one ever has to know I wasn't simply another forensics photographer."

With a furtive look around to make sure no one else was watching, the officer gave her a hesitant nod. "Okay. Just a quick look around, and don't touch anything, please."

"You're a star," Neveah told her. "Thank you, my dear. I'll be right back out, don't worry."

With a final bright smile over her shoulder, Neveah snagged a pair of sterile booties from a folding table that had been set up outside the perimeter and ducked beneath the yellow tape. A couple of people looked up at her, but as generally seemed to be the case in circumstances such as this, they assumed that because she'd received permission from the officer on duty to enter, it meant she was supposed to be there.

The restroom door on the back wall of the rustic building had been propped open. The room inside wasn't large, containing only a regular toilet stall and a handicapped-accessible stall across from the double sink and vanity. A hand dryer, a trashcan, and a diaper changing station completed the very standard setup.

A young man who been crouched on the dingy tile floor next to a faint bloodstain looked up when she poked her head in. His brow wrinkled in a frown as he took in the camera in her hands.

"They've already finished with the photos," he said.

She snapped a couple shots of the room's simple layout and sent him a sunny smile. "Not quite," she replied. "All done now, though. Thanks!"

It hadn't taken more than a second or two to detect the faint echo of magic lingering in the enclosed space. Not that it was truly a surprise. The likelihood that an apparent murder on the doorstep of the hidden passage connecting Earth to Hell was more than a simple human robbery gone wrong had been fairly high to start with.

The gateway to the demon realm had been quiet in the last several months, but things were still tense between the two powerful races. After all, they had only recently been at war with each other across dimensions. Earth might act as a sort of demilitarized zone between Hell and the Fae realm of Dhuinne — but these days, all it would take was one poorly timed diplomatic incident to start the whole repulsive business up again.

Unfortunately, a dead Fae lying at the literal gates of Hell *definitely* qualified as a diplomatic incident. Neveah couldn't imagine what the Fae woman had been thinking by even coming here in the first place. Her race might have been the nominal winners after the most recent intra-realm conflict, but they steered well clear of this place in the normal course of things.

This had the potential to be explosive. Neveah slipped beneath the crime scene tape and shucked off her disposable booties, sending the police officer a distracted nod of thanks. The woman beamed at her in return.

As she headed for the parking lot, she began plotting her next move. The humans would have taken the body to the nearest morgue for autopsy, and in an area like this that lacked any sort of entrenched Fae presence behind the scenes, the human doctors would have absolutely no idea what they were dealing with. As soon as she'd settled into the seat of her vintage VW Rabbit, she pulled out her phone and started dialing up contacts who would be able to help her discover which local hospital currently had a magic-infused corpse lying on a gurney in its basement.

TWO

"Baalazar, please tell me this is nothing more than an ill-judged jest," Nigellus said, kneading the bridge of his nose between his thumb and forefinger. He settled back in his chair with a sigh, giving his superior a severe look.

Like Nigellus, Baalazar was a demon of the first rank—a member of the ruling council in Hell. Unlike Nigellus, he seldom ventured outside of the demon realm. By contrast, Nigellus preferred to spend as much of his time as possible on Earth, despite the strictures on his interactions within the human world since the peace treaty between the Demons and the Fae had gone into effect a couple of centuries previously.

"Of course it's not a jest," Baalazar snapped. "Do you truly think I would joke about something so serious? The Fae prisoner has escaped from Hell, apparently with the help of that fool Leyak."

In his human guise, Baalazar was a fussy little man with dark hair and rounded shoulders. In his native demon form, he was an imp. He was also the fourth most powerful individual among the demonic host—ranked two steps above Nigellus, who preferred the relative freedom of being the lowest ranked member of the ruling Council of Six.

Nigellus closed his eyes for a moment and contemplated all of the ways the prisoner's escape could cause spectacular devastation.

"Let me call Edward in for this," he said. "Since you're doubtless about to charge me with finding your escapee — preferably before she can return to the Fae and tell them who's been keeping her prisoner for the last two hundred years."

Baalazar made an impatient gesture of assent with one pale hand. Nigellus reached for a bell rope hanging next to the small fireplace in the sitting room of his Atlantic City beach house. Distantly, the muffled sound of the bell reached them from the butler's pantry. A few moments later, Nigellus' soul-bound human servant entered the room.

"You rang, sir?" Edward asked, with the nearly undetectable hint of irony that colored most of his interactions with his demon master.

Edward had already been advanced in years for a human of his era when he'd sold his soul to Nigellus in exchange for success in his ill-fated life-long goal. When Edward's body finally began fail him at the age of eighty-four, Nigellus had taken him into service rather than reap his soul. It had been… a whim, really. A private bit of amusement, to make a servant out of a human who'd spent a lifetime seeking power.

The fact that he'd kept Edward around for the last several centuries was neither here nor there. They understood one another, to the extent that any human could understand what it meant to be an ageless and immortal demon. Besides, the man was occasionally useful for more than pressing shirts and dusting furniture.

"Edward," he greeted. "Baalazar has brought us unfortunate news. He's about to make his problem into my problem, which means I, in turn, am making it your problem."

"You do surprise me, sir," Edward replied, deadpan. Bushy white eyebrows drew together as he turned his rheumy hazel gaze on their guest. "Councilor Baalazar. May I ask the details of this unfortunate news?"

Baalazar's expression soured further. "A prisoner has escaped from Hell. It's vital that she be found and returned post-haste."

"Escaped from Hell?" Edward echoed. "She was demon-bound, then? Forgive me, but why not simply have the demon in question follow the trail of the soul-bond and retrieve her?"

It was a fair question, given that—in the vast majority of circumstances—a soul-bond would, in fact, act as a beacon. It would normally allow the demon holding the bond to teleport to the location of the bound individual, unless they were separated by a vast expanse of salt water or had been magically warded by an expert.

Baalazar huffed in frustration. "The demon in question is currently in at least four separate pieces. His heart and half his skull are still missing, meaning it will take some time before he's in a condition to do much of *anything* except lie there and twitch. The idiot." The last part was delivered in an irritated mutter.

Leyak would succeed in dragging all of his constituent body parts back eventually—assuming the prisoner hadn't thought to pack any of the important pieces in salt. Nigellus and his ilk were immortal in the truest sense of the word. They literally could not be killed. They could, however, be rendered temporarily helpless via the grisly means of dismemberment.

"Oh, dear. That's unfortunate," Edward said, in response to Baalazar's pronouncement. A look of alarm slid over his deeply lined features a moment later, as he evidently put two and two together. "Wait. This prisoner. It isn't—"

"It is," Nigellus confirmed dryly.

"The nameless Seelie warrior, yes," Baalazar snapped. "Hence the need to act quickly."

"I see," said Edward. "Yes, I suppose that's rather politically awkward, isn't it?"

"That is one way of putting it," Nigellus replied in a monotone.

The female Fae had wandered into Hell shortly after the end of the Last Great War, apparently with no memory of either her identity or her purpose in entering the demon realm. Since Fae were incapable of lying, it was assumed she'd been a survivor of some magical attack during the conflict that had left her mind permanently damaged.

The weak spot in the Veil that separated Earth and Hell functioned as a portal that only opened freely in one direction. It was located deep within a series of sprawling underground caverns in an area the humans now called California. Though it was invisible to the naked eye and the Demon's side was well guarded, there was nothing to physically prevent someone from stumbling through the gate.

The unlikelihood of anyone doing so by chance made the Seelie's story a bit suspect, but such a thing *had* actually occurred on a handful of occasions across the eons. The Council had been unwilling to allow one of their age-old enemies free run of Hell, but they'd gone so far as to make the Seelie's incarceration as pleasant as possible.

She couldn't leave without selling her soul to a demon—that was the nature of the gate between realms. And so, after much debate, the consensus had been that sending an amnesiac Fae captive back to Dhuinne, soul-bound to one of her mortal enemies, would have been more politically provocative than simply keeping quiet about the whole thing in hopes that her fellows would assume she'd been killed in battle.

Given the fragile peace that had reigned after the catastrophic closing days of the war, the decision made a certain amount of sense. Now, however, with the current political climate between the Demon Council and the Fae Court almost as fraught as it had been in those early days, it might be about to come back and bite them in a truly spectacular manner.

"The Fae realm is already undergoing political upheaval, with half the Court clamoring for a resumption of hostilities," Edward summarized. "And if your escaped Fae prisoner gets back to her people and tells them she's been an undeclared prisoner of Hell for the better part of the last two centuries, they're likely to use it as an excuse to tear up the treaty and burn the shreds to ashes."

"More or less," Baalazar agreed. "Therefore, we must find her before the Fae do. The alternative is unthinkable."

Edward's stooped shoulders rose and fell on a deep breath. "You realize that if she's magically adept, there's no reason to think she hasn't already portaled to the nearest ley line and traveled straight across the Atlantic to County Meath and the gate to Dhuinne."

Baalazar nodded. "Fortunately for us, in almost two hundred years, she's never shown any indication of being magically gifted to that degree. If she's reliant on non-magical travel, there is still a chance." The imp's granite-colored eyes flicked to Nigellus. "You've a property in Vallecito, located near the gate. Go there now and try to pick up the trail. I'll return to Hell and see if anything can be done to hurry Leyak's recovery along."

Nigellus nodded and swallowed a sigh, knowing that such a bounty hunt was unlikely to be simple. "Very well," he said. "I may need to contact you on short notice, though. Edward, have you a blade?"

Edward gave him a chiding look and pulled a small folding knife out of his pocket. As a human with some trifling natural facility for blood magic, he was seldom without one, and they both knew it. Nigellus took the tiny tool and thumbed it open, using its sharp point to nick the heel of his hand. Taking a handkerchief from his pocket, he pressed it to the bead of blood and passed the red-stained cloth to Baalazar before willing the wound closed.

The imp folded the fabric and slipped it into an inner pocket of his jacket, then accepted the knife and repeated the process with a kerchief of his own. Nigellus took both items from him and gave him a nod of farewell. Baalazar lifted his chin in acknowledgement and popped out of existence without another word.

The blood he'd spilled on the stained handkerchief tugged at Nigellus' awareness, a delicate, silken thread that would allow him to transport directly to Baalazar's side within a given realm. A few moments later, the sense of the connection weakened as the imp passed through Hell's gate.

Edward tilted his head, giving Nigellus a speculative look. "Well," he said. "Now I *know* you're concerned. You hate giving anyone tracking access like that. I take it we're off to California immediately, then?"

Nigellus' lips twisted in annoyance. "Apparently so. Cancel any appointments I have scheduled for the next few days and pack for us, please. The trail isn't growing any warmer."

***

The property in Calaveras County lay on a fertile slope outside of Vallecito, surrounded by vineyards. The house itself was warded within an inch of its life, for the sake of both privacy and security.

It was not Nigellus' preferred residence. Despite the other demons' bewilderment regarding his choice of a dwelling surrounded by salty ocean breezes, he favored the Atlantic City house. The Vallecito property was, however, useful for its proximity to the cave system the humans called the Moaning Caverns... and the gateway leading to his true home.

Magical wards made the property both invisible and unwelcoming to those who had not specifically been invited to breach them. They were no barrier to its owner, though—nor to Edward, who had crafted them using Nigellus' own power. The old human truly did have a knack for such jobs, his natural talents as a human warlock amplified by his access to a nearly bottomless well of demonic magic.

The house boasted a clean, minimalist design that Nigellus found agreeable, if only in small doses. Edward puttered around, checking all the rooms and plugging in the modem. While Nigellus didn't possess the patience to keep up with every new development in human technology, he did make a point of maintaining a basic familiarity with computers and the internet.

Once the Wi-Fi was turned on, he pulled out a sleek laptop and powered it up. One thing about the slow death of paper newspapers over the past couple of decades—it meant that even local news was accessible more quickly on the web than it would have been a few years previously. He began scanning the web for anything that looked as though it might be relevant. Unfortunately, Calaveras County consisted of tiny, mostly unincorporated towns that didn't run their own news sites.

"Try the police scanner," he called to Edward, before expanding his search to recent news stories containing the words 'Vallecito' or 'Moaning Caverns.'

"Of course, sir," Edward called back from the other room. "I suppose any reports of a confused woman in unusual clothing could be suggestive. Oh, and if nothing's coming up in a regular search on the news sites, check for recent tweets tagged with your keywords."

Unlike Nigellus, Edward was mildly fascinated by the technological trends of humans—another useful attribute in a servant. Nigellus grunted an acknowledgement and called up the relevant website. After a bit of poking and reordering, a tweet posted seven minutes earlier popped up from an account titled The Morning Watch. *Mysterious Death at Moaning Caverns Adventure Park in Northern California*, proclaimed the headline, followed by a shortened link leading to an external website and several hashtags including *#breaking-news* and *#exclusive*.

"Well spotted," he murmured and he clicked through.

Edward stuck his head in. "Find something already?"

"Quite possibly," Nigellus told him, his eyebrows climbing as he scanned the article on the independent news site.

Edward came in and read over his shoulder. "Good heavens. If your missing Seelie is already dead, that's a bit of a wrinkle, isn't it?"

Nigellus sat back in the desk chair, frowning.

"You don't think Leyak regained consciousness and reaped her soul?" Edward asked, his expression turning skeptical.

"If he did so without sanction from the Council, he's likely to spend the next few millennia occupying the same cell as his former captive, once Baalazar finds out," Nigellus replied.

"Hmm. Well, on the positive side, it should be a lot easier to track down a dead body than a living one who doesn't want to be found," Edward said philosophically.

Nigellus gave a wordless affirmative grunt, then shook his head slowly, crossing his arms over his chest. "Something's off about this."

"Garden-variety intuition, or demonic sixth sense?" Edward asked.

"The latter," Nigellus told him grimly, and made to rise. Edward stepped back to give him space.

Baalazar and Leyak were imps—drawing power from ambient magic attached to people and places. Nigellus, by contrast, was a demon of fate. He drew his power from the fabric of time, and like others of his ilk, it gave him a certain sense of when events were approaching a cusp of significance.

His servant exhaled a weary sigh. "Oh, good," he said. "Because *that* always goes well."

"Yes, *thank you*, Edward," Nigellus replied, already thinking ahead to what would be necessary when it came to gaining access to the body and disposing of it.

Edward reached down and started to snap the lid of the laptop closed, only to pause. "Er…" he began.

"What?" Nigellus glanced at him, frowning.

"I take it you didn't notice the byline," Edward said, turning the screen toward him.

Nigellus looked down at the name at the bottom of the article and stilled.

Neveah Lane.

Edward raised an eyebrow. "Isn't she the one who's—"

"Yes." Nigellus cut him off.

"—been stalking you for the past few years?" Edward finished.

Nigellus rubbed his temples.

"Coincidence?" Edward asked.

Nigellus shot him a sidelong look.

"Thought not," Edward murmured. "Right. I'll just go and start calling around to all the nearest hospitals, shall I?"

THREE

Morgues were a real downer, Neveah reflected. Even more so, now that she could relate to them — at least on a theoretical basis. Humans had been her first introduction to the concept of mortality; the idea that a sentient being could simply cease to exist. One day they were there, and the next, *poof*. No more human, just a human-shaped empty space in the world where they used to be.

After so many endless years spent trapped on Earth, the existence of death was no longer the novelty it had once been. She'd come to terms with the prospect that, at some nebulous future point in time, she, too, would be nothing more than a Neveah-shaped hole in reality. Eventually, in the absence of any connection to her home, the last of the energy that made her corporeal would dissipate into the ether, leaving nothing behind but a collection of online news articles and the transitory memories of other mortal beings.

So… yes. *Downer.*

However, morgues were also a good place to find individual dead bodies of interest, since humans in this part of the world seemed to be very invested in poking and prodding at fresh corpses to find out what had gone wrong with them before they died.

It had taken a bit of doing for her contact at *The Morning Watch* to find the right hospital, not to mention the travel time it took to drive here. She smiled pleasantly at the morgue attendant, a solidly built human in his late twenties who looked like he'd be capable of manhandling even the most recalcitrant dead person from the gurney to the cooler to the autopsy table.

"So, you see," she told him, "I just need a quick look at the body to confirm whether it's dear old Aunt Mary or not."

The man gave her a skeptical look, and she let a hint of her power leak out to bolster her case.

"Did you talk to the police already?" he asked. "Only, there's supposed to be an officer here with you to take down your statement in case you can identify the body."

"Oh, is there?" she asked, all innocence. "I'm so sorry—I must have misunderstood. I thought I was supposed to come here and then give a statement afterward."

The warmth of her invisible magnetic pull washed over the man, and he wavered, clearly fighting the urge to tell her things he shouldn't. She projected a bit more, hoping to tip him over the edge into speech.

"Well…" he began, hesitating. "The thing is, this particular case is a bit… *unusual*."

"Really? How so?" Neveah asked, wide-eyed.

The man licked his lips, struggling with himself for a moment before finally giving in. "It's the body. It keeps frying all our electronic equipment." The words came faster as he spoke, like they'd been piled up behind a dam and were spilling out through the cracks now that it had crumbled. "It's pretty crazy, if I'm being honest. We've got it stashed on *actual ice* because when we try and put it in the fridge with the other bodies, the circuit board in the thermostat shorts out and has to be replaced. Maintenance has been shitting bricks."

"Goodness. That *does* sound unpleasant," she said, wondering for the millionth time what possessed humans to come up with turns of phrase like that. "Anyway, if you can point me in the right direction, I'll only take a moment. Aunt Mary and I weren't particularly close, so you needn't worry about tears or hysterics."

"Right..." the attendant said uncertainly. She let her power slip its leash a tiny bit more, and he gave her a doe-eyed look of longing adoration before doing exactly as she'd asked.

They'd placed the body in a room that clearly hadn't been intended for storage of the dead. It was zipped into a standard black body bag, lying on a pile of ice in a large metal tub perhaps six feet long by three feet wide.

"You're sure you'll be all right in here on your own?" her guide asked, looking mildly disappointed when she nodded and thanked him.

Once the door closed behind him, Neveah reached down and pulled the zipper. As the two halves of the body bag parted, a haughty and beautiful face crowned by flaming red hair emerged. The woman's clothing had already been removed. A smear of dried blood marked her naked torso, but there was no wound beneath it—the body appeared unmarked, at least on the front side.

At this point, there was no question that the woman had been Seelie Fae. If Neveah's own senses hadn't already confirmed the flavor of the slowly dissipating magic in the gift shop restroom, the corpse's effect on human electronic equipment in the hospital would have been proof enough.

So. A dead Fae right on Hell's doorstep.

That was likely to be a problem. Possibly quite a large one.

Neveah's musings were interrupted by the sound of low voices outside. She straightened and turned to face the door to the room as it opened, a new brush of power tickling her senses. A striking figure stood silhouetted against the brighter lights of the hallway. And, *oh*, she recognized the scent of that power. Of course, given what she'd learned so far, it wasn't surprising that *he* would show up here.

It was Nigellus, the notorious spymaster of the Demon Council, who went by the rather disingenuous surname of Benecea on Earth. A demon of fate, and the strategic mind behind several of the more successful gambits during the last war. He was also an individual Neveah had been trying unsuccessfully to corner for some time, in hopes of getting some very specific questions answered.

Unfortunately, those questions might have to wait a bit longer, given the current situation.

"Mr. Benecea," she chirped, donning a layer of transparently false cheer and naiveté. "Fancy meeting you here! Have you come to identify poor Aunt Mary's body as well?"

"Ms. Lane," the demon replied, dry as the desert. "I wish I could say this is a pleasant surprise."

In his human guise, the demon was a tall man, though not outrageously so. His features were generally pleasing, though they might have been *more* pleasing if the bloody man ever cracked a smile. Eyes the color of fine bourbon assessed her coolly, set beneath swept brows and dark brown hair shot through with streaks of white at the temples.

Apparently he still maintained his penchant for very expensive tailoring, even while visiting a corpse. She wondered what his dry-cleaning bills were like.

"Believe me, it wasn't my intention to be predictable," she told him. "Though I suppose, since I'm a reporter and this is an exclusive news story, that is a *tiny* bit predictable. Tell me, did you steamroll that poor morgue attendant to get access to this room? Because, if you'll forgive me, that sounds dreadfully close to '*interference in human affairs.*' And I gather that's frowned on in some circles."

Specifically, in *Fae* circles—since demons had ceded control of the human realm to their old enemies as part of the peace negotiations.

"I'm sure I have no idea what you mean," he replied. "Please step aside, Ms. Lane."

Neveah stepped aside, curious as to how the demon would react to the corpse lying in a tub of ice. Nigellus moved to look down at the Fae woman's exposed upper body, his expression cold and calculating. Lifting one hand, he pressed a single finger to the gray-tinged skin of the Seelie's forehead and stood unmoving for a long moment, as though listening to something only he could hear.

"Well," he said, stepping back, "I suppose this is a simpler solution than the alternative."

With that, he reached out his right arm, fingers splayed open. An instant later, they closed around the hilt of a massive flaming sword that burst into existence out of nothingness. Neveah stared at the unearthly weapon in utter shock, her jaw hanging open.

"Are you—" she began, then cut herself off and tried again. "Is that…?"

But the demon of fate ignored her, his full attention on the Fae's remains. The sword dipped, its tip coming to rest over the Seelie's unbeating heart. The corpse and the body bag containing it flared with the same eerie flames surrounding the blade, and burned away to nothingness within seconds—leaving only melting ice behind.

Neveah continued to gape at him, her attention mostly on the fiery sword. He gave the weapon a final flourish, and it disappeared as suddenly as it had burst into existence. She dragged her gaze back to his face.

"I wasn't done examining that body! That was…" She sputtered in outrage, searching for appropriate words. "… *incredibly rude!*"

The demon didn't so much as break expression as he held her gaze, unblinking. The faintest hint of flickering red kindled in the depths of his pupils, and a wave of psychic power washed over her with undeniable force.

"Tell me what brought you here," he said, his tone growing resonant. "What have you learned about this woman during your investigations?"

The weight of the words pressed down on Neveah's mind, demanding an answer.

"Oh, a number of things," she replied without hesitation. "I always keep an ear to the ground for interesting happenings around the caverns, you know. Such a *fascinating* place, isn't it? When the police scanner for the area flagged a dead body in the gift shop restroom, I hopped in my car right away and drove over from Stockton. The victim was female and appeared to be in her early forties. She was also dressed in odd clothing and covered in blood—apparently not her own. I took some photos of the scene and did interviews with the staff and witnesses, of which there really weren't any good ones. Any good *witnesses*, that is to say. I'm sure the staff are fine."

Nigellus nodded, never breaking eye contact. "And what else did you learn?"

"Well, *here's* the really intriguing thing," Neveah continued eagerly. "The young lady who was watching the gift shop counter when the victim arrived is missing. She disappeared sometime before the police arrived. I have her cell phone number, but it just goes to voicemail, and her mailbox is already full. I haven't had a chance to follow up on that lead quite yet, but don't you find that interesting?"

"Perhaps," Nigellus said. "What is this young woman's name?"

"Alice Ramirez," she told him. "College student in Forestry and Natural Resources, rich parents, works at the adventure park during her summer vacations. I think that's pretty much everything that you don't already know about the case."

Nigellus nodded, thoughtful. "Very well. Your assistance is appreciated... if also mildly vexing." The weight against her mind grew heavier. "Now, you will forget this meeting, along with the disposition of the body. The staff will not question you or try to stop you when you leave. You will abandon your news story, and assume that the victim is an unknown Jane Doe whose identity and cause of death will never be determined."

Neveah scowled at him, dropping her cheerful demeanor abruptly. "Are you joking? Why in the name of heaven would I want to do *that*? You know, you're even ruder than I originally thought."

The demon blinked at her.

She pressed her lips into a thin line and glared back. "You've got a dead Seelie Fae right outside the gate to Hell. I think you've got way bigger problems than a news story published on an obscure indie website. So, maybe you'd better stop playing fast and loose with people's free will, and explain to me *exactly* what's been going on in the demon realm lately."

FOUR

"You're not human," Nigellus said slowly. "*Ah.* I suppose that does explain a few things."

Neveah rolled her eyes at him. "Is that really the conversation you want to have with me right now? You're holding a political hand grenade, and someone's just pulled the pin."

"Aptly put. Though I must say, you seem remarkably well informed for a contributor to an *obscure indie website,* as you put it." He was still watching her as though he expected her to jump in front of him and yell *boo.*

"Let's just say I've had a lot of time to do research," she said. "Are you staying in your invisible house? The one with all the grapes? If so, perhaps we could make a strategic withdrawal before someone outside shakes off your influence enough to wonder exactly what's going on in here."

He scoffed. "That's unlikely to be a concern. But yes, it might be prudent to retire somewhere a bit more comfortable for what could be a rather extended conversation." He extended a hand toward her. "May I?"

She tilted her chin in a regal nod. "Of course," she said, and placed her hand over his.

The world fell away in a dizzying whirl, the chilly and unpleasant atmosphere of the hospital morgue replaced in the blink of an eye by baking sun, moderated by a pleasant, late afternoon breeze. Neveah removed her hand and looked around, taking in the sights and sounds of nature. Birds chirped. Insects buzzed. Neat rows of grape trellises lined the slope of a hill a few hundred yards away.

She let the etheric fields flow across her senses, outlining the shape of a large but unseen object nearby. The concealment was expertly done, as were the spells layered over the building to repel anyone who might approach by mistake, convincing them that they wished to turn around and leave. She had no doubt there were additional magical tripwires in the area, crafted specifically to catch Fae.

"May I ask who did your wards?" she said. "I noticed the last time I was here that they're rather good."

He shot her a sidelong glance. "Really? As I recall, they didn't succeed at keeping *you* away from my door."

"Well, no," she agreed. "But then, they wouldn't, would they? I'm a bit of a special case."

She could practically feel the burn of his curiosity, but he only said, "To answer your question, my human servant crafted them. He prides himself on his expertise in such matters." With another hard look at her, he added, almost as an afterthought, "Neveah Lane, enter and be welcome."

The wards shimmered around her in response to his invitation, revealing the modern architecture that she'd been able to feel before, but not see.

"Classy," she said.

He made a noncommittal humming noise, keying in a security code at the front door and swinging it open. She vaguely remembered the sparkling white and metal decor from her previous visit—when she'd cornered him here in hopes of finally speaking to him, only to have the door slammed and locked unceremoniously in her face.

The house gave no indication of being lived in. It was picture perfect, staged as though for a real estate listing. She could detect no one else inside. "Is your servant here? Current crisis aside, I'd love to pick his brain about magical craft."

"Not presently. I believe he's following up some leads related to the 'current crisis,' as you put it." He ushered her into a high-ceilinged living room sparsely decorated with modern furniture.

She sat on a thin-cushioned ergonomic sofa and crossed her legs, regarding him as he settled onto the equally spartan chair across from her.

"Well, I suppose I finally know what it takes to get you to talk to me, at any rate. You've been quite a slippery one, Mr. Benecea." She raised an eyebrow. "Interesting choice of name, by the way. A corruption of 'blessed one'? Really?"

"It's as good a name as any other," he replied, steepling his fingers and studying her over them. "When one lives for long enough, one seeks fleeting amusement wherever it might be found."

Tell me about it, she thought.

38

"You seem quite remarkably well informed about other realms," he continued. "Yet you are not Fae, and you most certainly aren't demon. I confess myself intrigued."

She crossed her arms. "See, now, if you'd caught me a year ago, I'd have been thrilled to have that conversation with you," she told him. "But as things stand today, I'm a bit more concerned about the part where your people and the Fae are about to start trading metaphorical punches again, possibly flattening Earth in the process. I'm afraid the other subject might just end up being a distraction."

"A fair point," he said, giving nothing away.

She sighed in irritation. "So... maybe you'd like to explain why you decided to flambé the corpse before we could figure out exactly what happened to put it there in the first place?"

His expression grew calculating. "Not particularly, no."

"You really are the most infuriating—" she began, only to cut herself off with a sharp exhalation. "Fine, here's the deal, Nigellus of the Demon Council. Earth is the only home I've got left at this point, so I don't intend to see it turned into a giant sheet of volcanic glass after you lot start tossing magical bombs around."

"Nor do I," he said. "That's actually rather the point."

Neveah's people had once held a well-earned reputation for patience. Unfortunately, Neveah hadn't been a particularly good spokesperson for her race, even before things had gone pear-shaped.

Now, after a few thousand years kicking her heels among humans, she was even less inclined to put up with Nigellus's particular brand of stonewalling.

She retained very few of the gifts she'd originally possessed, but the power to inspire adoration was one she could still use. It took more energy than the resulting outpouring of love could replenish, but it was staggeringly effective in getting her what she needed, when she needed it.

Demons — immortal, ageless, and powerful though they were — had never been a match for Neveah's people. While she hadn't had cause to go head to head with one on this sort of battlefield before, she was confident that Nigellus would not be a match for her now.

The fate of three realms was at stake, and she wanted answers.

"You already know *exactly* how this Fae came to die on Hell's doorstep," she accused softly. Her power unfurled to its full extent, mantling around her like great wings, enveloping them both. "Tell me what's happening, spymaster. Maybe I can help you put the genie back in its bottle, assuming it's not already too late."

Nigellus' bourbon-colored eyes sharpened on her as her magnetic pull surrounded him. Hellfire sparked once more in their depths, stronger and brighter than before. She sensed his growing awareness of her gambit, as her aura demanded his immediate and reverent devotion. A human would've prostrated himself at her feet within the first two seconds. Nigellus fought the pull, his hands gripping the arms of his chair until the metal frame creaked in protest.

She wondered if anyone had ever turned his own mind games back on him before. Her race had fought his before humanity had even been a glimmer in evolution's eye, but they didn't engage in battles like this. Her fellows would have considered such manipulation beneath them — yet another unwritten rule that held no meaning for her now.

Nigellus rose from the chair, and she rose to match him.

"Tell me," she commanded, wrapping him up in her aura of love and pulling him closer to her.

He stumbled forward — another step, and another. Only when he was an arm's length away did she read the emotion behind his red-tinged eyes, and stop to wonder if perhaps there was *another* reason her people had never dallied with demons in quite this way.

Nigellus' hellish gaze didn't burn with uncontrollable adoration for her.

Instead, it burned with lust.

Oops, she thought, an instant before a long-fingered hand wrapped around her throat, walking her backward until her shoulders hit the nearest wall with a dull thud.

FIVE

"Oh, dear," she said, eyes wide as she looked up at the demon looming over her. "This wasn't quite what I had in mind."

"What *are* you?" Nigellus rasped. He took another aggressive step forward, insinuating a hard-muscled thigh between Neveah's legs.

A jolt of sensation shivered up her spine, the heart that she'd copied from the humans she lived amongst surging against the cage of her ribs. She swallowed convulsively, the movement pressing against the fingers spanning her throat.

"Ah. Well, you see..." she began, the words cut off in a gasp when the corded thigh between her legs sent another shudder of pleasure along her nerves. She wriggled, which turned out to be a less than successful strategy, assuming the goal was to escape the unaccustomed onslaught of physical pleasure.

That... had been the goal, right?

The demon's hard length pressed against the crease of her hip. He *growled*—a low, menacing rumble that Neveah felt straight to her core. In the bright light of the airy living room, she watched with wide eyes as curling ram's horns and great, leathery wings phased in and out of the current plane of existence like flickering images on film.

42

She was only distantly aware of the sound of a door being opened and closed.

"Sir?" came an unfamiliar human voice made rusty with advanced age. "Good heavens! *What* in the name of *sanity*?"

The subsequent blast of human magical force that jolted through them appeared to penetrate Nigellus' haze. He pushed away from the wall almost violently, his hulking demonic form phasing wildly back and forth with his urbane human guise.

"*Angel*," he hissed, as though it was a curse.

"Er, yes. Hello. Sorry about that," she managed, still trying to regain control of her galloping human senses. She lifted one hand, wiggling her fingers in a sheepish wave at the elderly human standing in the doorway. "You must be the wardsmith, right? Lovely to meet you."

The man regarded her with open consternation, cupping a ball of roiling magic energy in the palm of one gnarled hand. He was frail and stoop-shouldered, but his white, bushy eyebrows drew together above eyes that had seen battle before.

"Sir?" he asked the demon. "Are you well?"

Nigellus clenched his jaw and gave his shoulders a purposeful roll. The wings disappeared back to whatever dimension they normally resided in, as did the horns. Despite herself, Neveah kind of missed them.

"Yes, thank you, Edward," the demon said, as though they hadn't been openly rutting against each other mere seconds before. "Everything is under control."

The human—*Edward*—gave his master a mildly incredulous look, quickly masked. He flicked his fingers, dispersing the energy he'd held poised and ready to hurl.

"Oh, good," he said. "I trust you'll warn me if things are in danger of getting *out* of control, sir." He turned a wary gaze on Neveah. "Miss? I trust you're unharmed?"

"Oh, quite," she replied. "And please, you must call me Neveah. Mr. Benecea and I were just about to have a pleasant discussion about the dead Fae in the Moaning Caverns Adventure Park, but apparently the subject of conversation has just shifted a bit."

Nigellus regained himself enough to rejoin the discussion. "Your presence here is impossible. Heaven cut itself off from the other realms shortly after the war started."

Neveah winced. "Yes. They did. Bit of a long story, that."

Edward looked between them, gauging the atmosphere of the room. "Er… right. I'll just go and make drinks, shall I?" he said.

———◆———

A few minutes later, Neveah was once more seated on the couch—this time, with a glass of very passable red wine in one hand.

"Is this from the vineyard I saw outside?" she asked, swirling the crimson liquid and taking another sip.

"It is," Edward said, still sounding cautious.

44

"How lovely." She risked a quick glance at Nigellus, who was studiously ignoring the tumbler of whiskey cradled in his hands.

"You were about to explain what an angel is doing on Earth," the demon prompted, in a tone implying that if she hadn't been, she'd better start.

She let out a petulant sigh. "Yes. Well. You're quite right that Heaven slammed the gate closed on the other realms when it became clear the war between your people and the Fae was about to escalate. Unfortunately, they failed to do an accurate headcount first, and I was trapped on this side of the barrier when it snapped shut."

Nigellus stared at her for several seconds. "I thought you said it was a long story."

A sour expression tugged at the corners of her mouth. "Did I say that? Sorry, I meant 'embarrassing,' not long."

"You're saying you missed a memo from corporate and got locked out of Heaven?" Edward asked. "Was it just you, or are there other angels trapped on Earth?"

"Just me," she confirmed. "And I *did* say it was embarrassing."

"You've been alone on Earth for fifteen hundred years?" Nigellus asked. "And you have no contact at all with the angelic realm?"

"None," she said.

"How are you replenishing your power?" Nigellus demanded. "Angels draw directly from the fabric of their realm."

Discomfort trickled through her at the unwelcome reminder. This was not a subject she cared to discuss… or to think about at all, really.

"Mostly, I'm *not* replenishing it," she replied. "Angels have a deep reserve of power, but aside from the occasional bit of spontaneous love that comes my way, I've just been drawing down the metaphorical well across the years. Eventually I'll use the last of it and discorporate, I suppose."

She refused to dwell on the prospect of floating around the human realm as a diffuse, undifferentiated consciousness — still immortal, but cut off from everything that made existence worthwhile.

Nigellus raised an eyebrow pointedly. "You still have *some* angelic powers, clearly."

Neveah waved the words away. "Yes, yes. I'm one of the heavenly host. I can command adoration. But doing so uses more energy than it replenishes. I've already lost most of the rest of my angelic nature. I haven't been able to manifest my wings since the early nineteen-nineties." She shifted her shoulders uncomfortably against the back of the couch. "They *itch*."

The demon appeared mildly uncomfortable at that declaration — as, she supposed, would any winged being. Edward was already focused on other matters, however.

"And now you're a freelance internet reporter?" he asked.

She spread her hands in wordless affirmation.

"Why?" he pressed.

She gave the question a moment's consideration, because no one had ever asked before.

"What else would I do?" she replied.

The truth was, she'd merely been going through the motions for some considerable time now. The alternative was *not* going through the motions, and that sounded even worse. So, she poked her nose in where it wasn't wanted and wrote stories about the things she found out.

"I suppose it's also a useful career when it comes to stalking someone." Nigellus' tone was pointed.

"Yes, that too," she agreed. "Though you've been an exceptionally slippery target, up until now."

"Why stalk him in the first place, though?" Edward asked.

She snorted. "Why stalk the one member of the Demon Council with an established presence on Earth? Forgive me, but who else would I consult about the barrier protecting Heaven from the other realms? The Fae know nothing about it, and they care even less."

Understanding dawned on the demon's tightly controlled features. "You still wish to go back."

"Of course I wish to go back!" she said. "Do you think I *want* to rattle around this ridiculous planet until I'm nothing more than an incorporeal consciousness floating on the breeze?"

Most humans weren't even aware of the world beneath the world. They bumbled around, never realizing that Earth had been the spoils in a war they knew nothing about. At least the vampires had been *interesting*... and then the demons had gone and let most of them become cannon fodder during the conflict.

"I see," Nigellus said. "And what of your involvement with this current crisis?"

"You mean your dead Fae?" she asked. "I don't *have* any involvement in the 'current crisis,' beyond what you already know. I'm a reporter; I keep close tabs on the area around the gate to Hell. I also have a vested interest in making sure Earth doesn't get flattened by the more powerful races—since, as I've already made clear, I'm stuck here."

"When it comes to the matter of Earth's safety, we are, in fact, in accord," Nigellus said. "Restarting the war is to no one's benefit."

She sat back on the couch, absently twirling the stem of the empty wine glass between her finger and thumb. "Tell me something, in that case."

His wary look returned.

"You wield an angelic sword," she said. "How did you come by it?"

One dark eyebrow quirked. She'd surprised him.

"Shemasiel's sword?" he replied. "I bartered a favor to another demon in exchange for it, some centuries ago."

"And where did they get it?" she asked.

"I've no idea," Nigellus said. "My understanding is that it has changed hands several times since it was originally captured in battle during the angelic wars. Why?"

She consciously let it go. "It's not important. I was just curious." With a deep breath, she moved on to a more important subject. "Tell you what, why don't we discuss the fact that a random human college student is the main suspect in the killing of a Fae warrior, instead? Because I'm sorry, but that doesn't track."

Edward's bushy eyebrows drew together. "It certainly doesn't. What random human are we talking about?"

Neveah filled him in on Alice Ramirez and her abrupt disappearance around the time of the death.

"Alice from the gift shop?" Edward asked, clearly taken aback. "Oh, *heavens*, no. She's worked there every summer since she graduated high school. She couldn't have done it."

"You are both correct," Nigellus said once she'd finished. "No human killed that Fae without a struggle, and without leaving a single mark on the body. There must be some other explanation. Perhaps Ms. Ramirez came upon the corpse and panicked."

"Which means there would have to be some *other* explanation for a Seelie warrior dropping dead in a gift shop restroom," Neveah pointed out. "There's something important you're not telling me about this situation, *spymaster*."

He tilted his head. "It's intriguing that you would expect otherwise."

Edward had been following the exchange like someone watching a tennis match. "Well, sir," he said. "Forgive my impertinence, but if you can't trust an angel…"

Nigellus glared at him.

"And it's not as though you appear to be making great strides in uncovering the mystery on your own," Neveah added. "At least, not beyond flambéing the evidence. Fortunately for you, despite being a terrible example of an angel, I'm a rather good example of an investigative reporter."

Edward gave his employer a narrow look. "You flambéed the body, sir? Really?"

Nigellus scowled. "I *disposed* of the body, which ensures that it will not end up falling into the hands of the Fae. That was rather the point of all this—and normally, I would be inclined to report back that the matter has been dealt with... except for the small remaining mystery of this missing human woman."

Neveah gave a slow, predatory smile. "So the dead Fae is someone who won't be missed? That's an interesting tidbit. Where might she have come from, I wonder, that none of her people would be looking for her?"

Edward rubbed at the bridge of his beaky nose. "You might as well tell her, sir. She's going to figure it out regardless, and she's right that we could use the help."

The demon's expression went blank, betraying nothing.

Neveah huffed in irritation. "You already said it yourself. Despite appearances, if your goal is to maintain the peace, we're on the same side. Earth is the only home I've got left."

Nigellus regarded her with a piercing gaze, and it occurred to her that this whole meeting could have gone a *bit* more smoothly.

"Are you certain you wouldn't prefer to drag the information directly from my mind?" he asked, with misleading mildness.

She frowned at him. "Uh, *hello*? Pot, kettle? Is that really the moral high ground you want to battle over?"

"Moral high ground isn't generally the purview of demons. But your point is taken." He paused, exhaling slowly through his nostrils. Grudgingly, he continued, "And, on that note, the answer you seek is that the dead Seelie woman wandered into Hell shortly after the peace treaty was struck—allegedly with no memory of either her identity or her purpose in coming there. She has been a… *guest*… of ours ever since."

Puzzle pieces rearranged themselves inside Neveah's head. "Oh," she said. And then, "*Oh*. Oh, dear."

"Quite," Nigellus agreed.

Implications fell one by one like dominoes. "This Fae *escaped Hell*? Where is the demon she was bound to?"

"Currently in several unattached pieces," Nigellus said dryly.

She winced. "Ouch. I guess he's not going to have a good time of it with the Council once he pulls himself together."

"That's putting it mildly," Edward muttered.

"And you never found out who the Seelie was?" Neveah asked. "The Fae Court never missed her, or came around asking questions?"

"Never," Nigellus confirmed.

She mulled that over for a bit.

"So, assuming Alice Ramirez was just an innocent bystander who panicked at the sight of a dead body, you're free and clear. The Fae weren't looking for her before, and there's no corpse to act as a smoking gun, so there's no reason for them to suspect anything."

"One can only hope for a world that simple," Nigellus said. "But if, as you suggest, there is more to Ms. Ramirez' involvement…"

"Then you're still potentially in trouble," Neveah finished. "She could say something to the wrong person, and it could get back to one of the Fae who oversee things on Earth behind the scenes."

Nigellus tilted his head in acknowledgement.

"*Well.*" Neveah set the empty wine glass on the arm of the sofa and clapped her hands together briskly. "We've got a full name, a cell phone number, a city of residence, and a current college enrollment. It sounds like we'd better track down a street address and go pay Alice's apartment a visit. If nothing else, her poor parents will be worried out of their minds when they find out she's missing."

SIX

Tracking down people of interest was well within Neveah's purview as a reporter, and it also turned out that Nigellus' demon-bound servant had a surprising affinity with technology, given his age. It didn't take long to get an address and apartment number for Alice Ramirez using publicly available websites.

Edward elected to remain behind, searching for additional news articles related to the death or the disappearance of the body. So far, aside from a couple of mentions of odd clothing, there was nothing to flag the incident as anything other than a miscellaneous human tragedy. If Nigellus had done a competent job of covering his tracks at the hospital by influencing the minds of the morgue staff, there was no reason to think the Fae would ever hear about it.

Hopefully, that would be the end of it. Earth had come under nominal Fae control after the treaty went into effect, and the Fae presence behind the scenes of the human political and military structure was extensive. The ruling Court in Dhuinne was additionally undergoing its own brand of political upheaval, after a prominent Unseelie member was found to be engaging in a treasonous plot.

Even so, when it came to the human realm, the Fae weren't omniscient. Woe betide any individual human or vampire who came into their cross-hairs—but they weren't running 24/7 surveillance on every corner of the globe. Additionally, Fae and advanced human technology didn't get along terribly well. Their magic tended to fry anything with a circuit board unless they actively shielded their auras, as the IT department in the hospital had discovered the hard way.

Combine that fact with their reluctance to poke around too close to the stronghold of their old enemies the demons, and it was quite possible this entire thing would end up flying completely beneath their radar. At least, assuming Alice Ramirez didn't become an unexpected glitch in the proceedings.

Neveah tamped down any lingering mortification at being alone in a car with Nigellus as the demon drove them into Vallecito. There wasn't much to the tiny town. A post office; a historic monument located in front of a small church. The nearest amenities were a couple of miles away in the slightly larger town of Angels Camp. Most of the houses were modest single-family dwellings— some neatly kept, others with makeshift wood and sheet metal fences, or cars up on blocks in the yard.

Alice Ramirez lived in a rare triplex located a couple of blocks from the high school. It was a sprawling structure that gave the impression of having been cobbled together over the course of several decades, rather than designed from the beginning as a multi-family unit. The outside was painted a cheerful yellow color, and scraggly flow-erbeds lined the edge of the yard. Each unit had its own driveway, and a 'For Rent' sign stood haphazardly next to the center unit's driveway.

An old Buick sedan sat in front of the first unit, and there was no car in the third unit's driveway.

"Apartment C," Neveah said, pointing to the empty drive.

Nigellus pulled his dark blue Maserati Quattroporte into the empty space and turned off the engine. Neveah had tried very hard not to scoff upon seeing the ridiculous sports car—but in the demon's defense, she could hardly make a joke about him needing to compensate for anything after the scene earlier in his living room.

A small furrow formed in his brow as he stared at the door to the unit.

"Something's off," he said.

Neveah stretched her senses outward as best she could, but could feel nothing out of the ordinary. "What do you mean?"

He gave a small shake of the head. "It's faint, but time's turning is twisted up in this place. Something of significance has happened, or is about to happen."

She eyed him for a long moment before reaching for the door handle. "I bet demons of fate are a lot of fun at parties."

Unlike imps, who drew power from free magic floating in the ether, or succubi and incubi, who drew power from the animus of living things, demons of fate drew directly from the fabric of reality. It didn't mean they could see the future or predict specific occurrences, but it did tend to make them sensitive to unusual events. In the current context, that didn't bode particularly well.

There was nothing for it but to go up and knock. Neveah did, aware on a visceral level of the demon lurking behind her. This, she suspected, was what humans meant when they talked about the hair on the back of their necks standing up. He would only have to take a single step forward and —

"No answer," she said unnecessarily, cutting off that line of thought before it could take root.

Nigellus reached past her and grasped the doorknob, pushing the door sharply inward. With a splintering sound, the metal lock plate tore free of the frame, and the door swung free.

"Subtle," Neveah observed. "So, I take it you consider the 'no interference in human affairs' clause of the peace treaty to be more of a suggestion than a hard and fast rule?"

"This is very much a demon affair, not a human one." He sauntered inside, looking around the homey space. "If I can prevent it from also becoming a Fae affair, I expect the Council will allow me some latitude on the matter."

Neveah squeezed in past him, also examining Alice's living area. They split up in wordless accord, Nigellus heading toward the kitchen, while Neveah followed a short hallway to the single bedroom.

The closet door was standing open, and the bed was unmade — which could be relevant, or could merely indicate that a human college student lived here. However, the set of luggage jammed into the space between the bed and the wall argued for the former. It was the kind that could be stored like Russian dolls, with the carryon nested inside the midsize suitcase, which in turn fit inside the largest suitcase.

Except the carryon was missing.

She ducked across the hall to check for the presence or absence of a toothbrush and toiletries in the bathroom, only to stop cold upon opening the door.

Footsteps sounded against the hardwood floor at the far end of the hallway.

"It's very faint, but there's a trace of Fae magic lingering in this place," Nigellus called. "There's also a forty-pound bag of water softener salt in the kitchen, which is potentially suggestive. Have you found anything of interest?"

"I suppose you could say that." Her skin prickled again as the demon came up behind her. She took a step to the side within the cramped space, revealing a limp, wrinkled arm protruding through the gap at the edge of the shower curtain.

"*Ah,*" Nigellus said.

* * *

Shoulder to shoulder, they stared down at the bloodied remains of an older human woman wearing a floral print housedress. The cause of death was obvious enough—her throat had been slit from ear to ear.

"The attacker dragged her into the tub before killing her," Neveah observed. "Look at the pattern of blood spray on the walls."

"Agreed." Nigellus sounded grim, as well he might. "So much for a neat resolution to the issue."

That was putting it mildly. Nothing about the sequence of events made sense.

Neveah blew out a frustrated breath. "We have a random female college student who is apparently also a cold-blooded killer, and just happened to be present shortly before the death of a Seelie warrior powerful enough to escape Hell and dismember the demon she was bound to." She dragged her attention away from the body in favor of checking the vanity and medicine cabinet. "Our girl's made a run for it, too. There's a carryon bag missing, along with her toothbrush and toothpaste."

"Wait here a moment," Nigellus said. "I'd like to check something in the other occupied apartment."

He left without another word, leaving her alone with the body. Neveah crossed to the tub and gazed down at it for a moment longer. She pulled the shower curtain closed, just as it had been before, and headed for the kitchen. As Nigellus had mentioned, there was a plastic forty-pound bag of salt pellets propped in the corner next to a cabinet. The top had been messily cut open, and perhaps a quarter of the contents were gone. Nothing else in the room appeared out of place.

Nigellus returned in short order, a frown on his striking features as he typed rapidly on his phone.

"The door to the other unit was unlocked," he said without looking up. "There were several old photographs in the apartment, including some of the dead woman. That's where she lived, apparently alone. I examined her mail to get the name, and according to the county assessor's database—which I've just checked—she owned this building."

He looked up and put the phone away.

Neveah mulled that over. "So, picture this scenario. The police come and knock, looking for Alice, but they haven't got a warrant to search the place yet. She's either not here or she doesn't answer, and they leave. The landlady comes over, wanting to know why law enforcement is knocking at her tenant's door, and she gets her throat slit for her troubles. After which, Alice high-tails it out of here with her carryon."

"I suppose it fits all of the facts, if one ignores the cognitive dissonance surrounding the young female college student being a vicious murderer." Nigellus jerked his chin toward the open bag in the corner. "There is also the salt."

"Maybe the building's water softener system needed recharging?" Neveah suggested without enthusiasm. She shook her head, dismissing it for now. "There's one other thing I want to check before we leave. She has a safe in her bedroom closet. It looks cheap enough to be easily crackable, and there might be some useful information inside."

"Such as?" Nigellus asked.

Neveah shrugged. "I won't know until I see it, will I? But if there's a passport inside, that would imply she's not planning on leaving the country.

Or if there's anything hinting at previous illegal activity, it could give us some insight into her sudden bloodthirstiness."

Nigellus shot her a narrow look. "You can't genuinely believe this human woman killed a Seelie warrior?"

She spread her hands. "I have *literally no idea*. I'm trying not to make assumptions about any of it."

The demon appeared unconvinced, but he followed her to the bedroom where the little safe sat on a shelf in the corner of the closet. Neveah examined the simple combination lock, leaning close as she gave it an experimental spin.

"I can force that, if you're truly set on seeing the contents," Nigellus said.

She shook her head and waved at him for quiet. "No need."

Tilting her ear toward the mechanism, she turned the lock a click at a time, listening for the tumblers to fall into place one by one. In only a couple of minutes, the last one fell. Neveah looked up in triumph, but Nigellus was at the bedroom window, staring out.

"There are police cars approaching," he said. "That warrant may have come through. Time to leave."

"Just a second—I've cracked it," Neveah replied, grasping the handle and pulling the safe door open. An explosion of sound hit her at the same time as a massive impact in the center of her chest. She staggered backward and hit the floor hard, unable to breathe past the fiery pain radiating outward from her shattered sternum. Gray splotches gathered at the corners of her vision.

"*Angel!*" Nigellus called sharply.

He'd been right across the room, she was certain of it—but for some reason, he suddenly sounded very far away.

SEVEN

Nigellus whirled away from the window in response to the deafening sound of a single gunshot, just in time to see the angel stumble back and collapse to the floor with a neat hole in her chest.

"*Angel!*" he called, crossing the room in less than a second and falling to his knees beside her.

The safe stood open, a faint curl of smoke coming from the muzzle of a high caliber semi-automatic handgun mounted inside. A piece of string tied to the door suggested the mechanism of action—the other end of the twine attached to the trigger and ran through a pulley at the back.

Neveah lay on the ground, clutching feebly at her chest and conspicuously failing to heal. Outside, the squeak of automotive brakes announced the arrival of the police.

"Control your bleeding," Nigellus snapped. "The last thing we need is angelic blood ending up in a human forensics lab."

He'd hoped to dispose of the elderly human's body and clean up the crime scene, in an attempt to prevent the human authorities from expanding the investigation surrounding Alice Ramirez. He'd also hoped *not* to leave an expensive car indirectly registered to his human servant sitting in the driveway of the apartment.

"Police! We have a warrant to search the property!" The muffled declaration filtered to him through the broken front door.

Apparently, the universe had other ideas.

He took a precious couple of seconds to confirm that there was nothing in the safe except the gun, before crouching once more at the angel's side and clasping a hand around her arm. She stared up at him, mouth open like a fish gasping air instead of water.

She should be healing by now.

He could allow the police to enter and overpower them mentally, rearranging their minds and memories to suit his bidding. But that would take time, and the angel had a bullet hole through her heart that wasn't regenerating properly.

There *was* no time.

"Brace," he warned her, and wrenched them sideways through the ether.

They reappeared in one of the lavish bathrooms of the winery house. The juxtaposition of the bloody human body in Alice Ramirez' bathtub and the bleeding angel on his white tile floor was disconcerting.

"Edward!" he bellowed, releasing Neveah's arm in favor of ripping open the front of the conservative blouse she was wearing. He snapped the band of the bra beneath, and her breasts bounced free. With a low growl of irritation, he shoved aside the faint echo of the unnatural lust she'd planted in his mind, which still hadn't dissipated. The bullet wound that had shattered her sternum oozed blood sluggishly.

She whimpered as he eased a hand beneath her shoulders and lifted her upper body, searching for an exit wound. There wasn't one.

Familiar footsteps approached.

"Sir? What—" Edward came to an abrupt halt inside the doorway. "Good lord. Dare I ask what happened?"

"A booby trap," he said succinctly. "A single large-caliber round admirably aimed for the heart. It appears the bullet is still inside her, though her body should have expelled it and healed almost instantaneously."

"Too weak... for that," she wheezed, the words a bare rasp.

Edward blinked once and settled into practicality. "She's still immortal. She won't die, and that bullet wants taking out, as a first step."

"Agreed," the angel croaked.

"Agreed," Nigellus echoed dryly. "I trust there's an appropriate blade somewhere in the kitchen?"

"I expect so," Edward said. "Back in a tick."

He hurried off.

"Can you tell where the bullet is lodged?" Nigellus asked the angel, still supporting her upper body. Her skin felt feverish against his splayed hand, even through the fabric of her torn clothing.

"Left... clavicle," she managed.

He nodded. "It will be easier to go in from the back."

Her nose wrinkled. "Maybe... for... you..."

He couldn't help reflecting what an utterly unexpected creature she was. Long, white-blonde hair framed an elfin face dominated by eyes the color of a clear summer sky on Earth. She should be a powerful being of legend, but her weakness leant her an air of almost human vulnerability. Misleading, of course. She'd overpowered his mind with startling ease before—though not, he gathered, in precisely the way she'd intended.

Fortunately for you, despite being a terrible example of an angel, I'm a rather good example of an investigative reporter, she'd said, and so far, it appeared she at least possessed the gift of self-awareness.

Edward returned bearing a vicious looking, narrow-bladed boning knife and an entire bottle of whiskey. Nigellus raised an eyebrow at him and he gave an unrepentant shrug in return.

"Is this any use for your metabolism, Ms. Lane?" he asked, lifting the bottle.

"Maybe, if I'm weak enough," she rasped, reaching for it.

Edward removed the cork and handed it to her, helping her support the bottle as she drank. Nigellus assumed she'd have refused it if the bullet had done any catastrophic damage to her esophagus. Idly, he wondered how much detail she'd adopted in crafting her human form.

After downing perhaps a third of the bottle, she drew back, and Edward took it away.

"Okay," she said. "Get it over with."

Nigellus helped her out of her blouse and bra before easing her forward to drape her arms over the edge of the jetted bathtub so she could steady herself.

"Who puts a loaded gun in a safe as a booby trap?" she muttered, wincing as she settled in.

He took the knife from Edward and knelt behind her. "A murderous college student, apparently."

Edward lowered himself on creaky knees to perch on the edge of the tub next to the injured angel. He extended a hand to her, and after a moment's hesitation, she took it. Nigellus resigned himself to the possibility that he would need to mend broken bones in his servant's hand before all was said and done, but the human made his own choices when it came to such small acts of kindness.

This whole thing would have been considerably easier if he'd been comfortable using magic to force the bullet out of the angel's body. But despite her protestations of weakness, he didn't trust how her own powers would react to his.

There was nothing else for it. With his free hand, he palpated around the clavicle, searching out the hint of lead with his deeper senses. It was lodged beneath the medial edge of the bone, and there was another unwelcome substance present, as well.

That was going to further complicate matters — as if they weren't complicated enough already.

"So, I take it hopes for a neat solution to all of this are pretty well dashed, sir?" Edward asked, as though reading his thoughts.

"Thoroughly," he replied, and brought the blade to bear with as much delicacy as he could muster.

The angel made a tiny, trapped-prey noise, but did not flinch. Nigellus opened an incision just large enough that he could reach a finger inside and hook the offending bullet out of her body. It burned like acid from the first touch, and he tossed it into the basin of the bathtub as though it were red hot. It landed with a metallic clink.

A thin trail of smoke wafted up from his scorched finger and thumb, the smell of burning flesh tickling his nose.

Edward scowled and reached down to retrieve the lead pellet—now deformed into a shape resembling a flower's open petals.

"I smell something burning. What just happened?" Neveah asked weakly.

"Salt?" Edward said, directing the question at Nigellus, who nodded.

"You were shot with a hollow point bullet," he told the angel. "One packed with salt crystals."

"Oh," Neveah said after a short pause. "That's... rather alarming."

She wasn't wrong.

He took a moment to direct enough magical energy to heal the burned skin of his fingers before asking, "Do you want this wound cauterized? You're still not healing properly."

"Yes, please," Neveah said, sounding exhausted. "It's taking an awful lot of concentration to keep the blood inside as it is."

"Very well," he told her, and heated the blade to red-hot with a thought. "Hold still."

She held still, muscles tense beneath creamy skin as he pressed the blade to the small incision he'd just made, and held it there until the wound was sealed. The entrance wound was not as neat, but he closed it as best he could. Beyond a hiss of discomfort, she didn't comment.

Edward, who had apparently avoided any crushed fingers while holding her hand, rose and retrieved a robe from the row of hooks behind the door. He helped her slide it over her shoulders and stepped back to let her tie it around her waist. The brilliant white terrycloth practically swallowed her petite frame.

She looked up at Nigellus, gray-faced and wan. "That bullet was meant for a demon."

"Yes," he agreed grimly.

Had she taken him up on his offer to force the safe open, *he* would have been the one shot through the chest by a bullet containing the one substance to which demons were vulnerable. It wouldn't have killed him—nothing could kill an immortal— but salt in the heart or the brain was without a doubt the most painful injury a demon could sustain.

"You should rest, Ms. Lane," Edward said. "May I show you to a guest room?"

She rose unsteadily. "I'm afraid angels don't sleep—no more than demons do. But if you'll give me the rest of that whiskey, I'll see if I can at least manage drunken unconsciousness for a bit." She poked gingerly at her chest. "I have to say, I'm really not enjoying this at all."

"Indeed not, miss," Edward agreed. "Right this way, please. The room isn't far."

He retrieved the whiskey bottle and the angel, ushering her toward the door and matching his pace to her slow, hitching one.

"I must return to Miss Ramirez' apartment to get the car back and ensure it isn't traced," Nigellus told their retreating backs. "I'll be as quick as I can."

"Of course, sir," Edward agreed, supporting their injured angelic guest with a hand beneath her elbow.

———◆———

The Maserati was still in Ms. Ramirez' driveway when Nigellus teleported back to the cheery yellow triplex, his mind awash with the implications of this latest revelation.

The temptation to interfere with the police investigation was difficult to ignore. He would have to do so, to some extent—since making certain the authorities didn't trace the car back to Edward was non-negotiable. But as for the rest of it, things were already ballooning to a degree that would be nearly impossible to contain—at least, not without planting a number of big red flags emblazoned with the words *'warning: demon interference.'*

The humans themselves might not make the connection to supernatural influence if he succeeded in completely covering up the landlady's murder. However, any Fae poking around the investigation assuredly *would* make the connection—and at this point, such a prospect was still moderately worse than the prospect that they'd come poking around the investigation *without* finding evidence of demonic interference on Earth.

There were too many loose ends. The landlady's body itself... any forensic evidence that had already been photographed and sent off... the discharged gun in the safe... the existing records related to Alice Ramirez' disappearance after the death of the escaped Fae prisoner. There were likely to be dozens of human investigators either directly or peripherally involved already, and any one of them could raise the alarm if evidence—much less another corpse—went missing.

Out of all of it, the salt-laced bullet was the part he found most alarming. Alice clearly knew about the supernatural world, and not only that—she'd expected it to show up inside her apartment. She knew about demons and their one weakness, *and she shouldn't.* The only conceivable explanation he could come up with was that she was a Fae operative... but if that were the case, how did the dead Seelie fit in?

He set his musings aside in favor of dealing with the blasted Maserati.

Two forensic techs were dusting the vehicle for fingerprints when he walked up. A thankless task, since neither demons nor angels possessed dermal papillae on their fingertips. Fortunately, Edward never drove the car, preferring the Aston Martin when they were staying in this area.

He hooked the two men's gazes as they looked up in response to his approach, letting his power wrap around their thoughts. "You're finished with your task. You didn't find anything of use," he said, saving them the trouble. "Tell me who called in the license number, please."

They gaped at him for a moment, before the nearest tech raised a hand to point through the open apartment door. "It was Lieutenant Walker."

"Thank you," he said, and walked into the apartment.

A man in a poorly fitting suit looked up and frowned, raising a hand in the universal gesture for *stop*. "Whoa, whoa, whoa. Who the hell are you? This is an active crime scene, buddy!"

Several other people looked up as well. Nigellus let his power flow through the room.

"Lieutenant Walker? I'm here to take the vehicle to impound," he said calmly. "Dark blue Mazda 626, license plate number 6LBK274."

The man in the suit blinked at him. "What? No, it was… it was a… Maserati?"

"No," he repeated. "It was a dark blue Mazda 626, license plate number 6LBK274. Someone made a mistake taking down the information earlier. You should call in the correction right away."

The lieutenant stared at him for a long moment, blank-faced and open-mouthed. Nigellus stared back, and the man took out his phone and dialed. He waited until the lieutenant finished speaking to the person on the other end and hung up, returning the phone to his pocket.

"Just a simple mistake," the human muttered. "Could happen to anyone."

"Quite so," Nigellus agreed. "Now, if someone could move the squad car blocking the end of the driveway?"

A uniformed officer nodded dumbly and squeezed past Nigellus to go outside. Again, Nigellus resisted the urge to plant any other seeds in the humans' minds, since that might easily come back to haunt him later if he miscalculated in the slightest.

"Thank you, Lieutenant," he said instead, and went to take the Maserati back to the house.

He arrived to find Edward waiting for him.

"You should have let them keep the bloody car," his servant greeted. "They probably wouldn't have been able to sort out the ownership through all the various shell corporations, and you could have replaced it with a convertible *because we're in bloody California.*"

Nigellus gave him a long look. "You're upset about something. I assume it's not really regarding the Masersati."

Edward pressed his lips together, visibly mastering himself. "Sir. There is an *angel* in your guest room. An angel, I might add, who is currently collapsed in a drunken stupor from a salt-laced bullet wound intended for a demon... and she isn't healing."

"Still?" Nigellus asked, suppressing a tiny twinge of alarm. "She should have begun regenerating by now, even if she's weakened."

"Yes," Edward agreed with forced patience. "She should have. That's rather the point I'm trying to make. Though I would also like to return to the 'intended for a demon' part, if we could. Why was there a booby trap involving salt in this young woman's apartment? How could she possibly have known to expect a visit from a demon... much less known how best to attack one?"

"All good questions," Nigellus replied. "There was also a large bag of salt in her kitchen, with perhaps eight or ten pounds missing."

Edward's bushy eyebrows shot up. "And you didn't think to mention this earlier?"

Nigellus gave him a flat stare. "I was somewhat distracted."

The human huffed. "That's one way of putting it... *sir.*"

Nigellus was *not* going to acknowledge that his elderly human servant had snapped him out of a bout of angelically induced lust. If he did, he'd never live it down.

They stared at each other, daring the other to blink. Edward broke first, with a put-upon sigh. "Very well. It seems we have both a dead Fae and a would-be demon hunter to deal with, in that case. First, though—how are we going to power up an angel who's cut off from Heaven? Because even if it was an unintentional sacrifice—she took that bullet for *you*, sir."

Nigellus closed his eyes and rubbed at them. "Yes. I suppose she did. So the question becomes, where does one go on Earth to experience a large upswelling of spontaneous love from strangers?"

EIGHT

Neveah emerged from a state of hazy half-awareness to find herself still in Nigellus' guest bedroom, and still in pain. The sky beyond the window was dark, but someone had left a single lamp on its dimmest setting in the far corner of the room.

That had been thoughtful, if unnecessary. Probably Edward's doing.

She eased out of the comfortable bed, wincing as her body protested. There was a mirror above the dresser. Tugging the edges of the robe apart, she leaned forward to examine the scorched entrance wound in her chest. The edges of the flesh were finally starting to pull closed, but even that small amount of healing was drawing on resources she barely possessed anymore. Her skin looked pale to the point of translucency.

A sense of dread rose up as she contemplated the clear signs that her hard-used human-ish body was fraying at the seams. It had served her well for millennia… but then again, she hadn't gone around standing in front of high-speed metal projectiles for most of that time.

A light knock sounded against the wood of the closed bedroom door. She retied her borrowed robe and went to open it. Nigellus stood outside, impeccable in Armani with the top two buttons of his cranberry-colored shirt undone. The upper edge of a tattoo was just visible above his collar—three crosses, arranged in the standard depiction of the Christian crucifixion.

"Hello," she said. "Your alcohol is excellent, by the way. At least, I assume it is. I'm not usually much of a drinker."

"If one is to indulge in vice, it might as well be high-quality vice," he replied. His eyes—the same amber color as the whiskey had been—played over her, assessing. She tried not to shiver under that unyielding gaze. "Your reserves are depleted. I'm taking you someplace that might help."

She stared at him in momentary incomprehension, her brain sloshing around in the remnants of the alcohol like a pickled egg. "Are you?"

"Yes," he said with forced patience. "You live in Stockton, I believe you said?"

"That's right."

The demon nodded. "I took the liberty of retrieving your... car... from the hospital parking lot."

He hesitated over the word, as though uncertain it was the correct noun to describe her vintage diesel Rabbit.

"How did you know which one was mine?" she asked.

"Your power signature is all over it." He tilted his head, still watching her closely. "Though admittedly somewhat overpowered by the stench of used french fry grease."

"It has a vegetable oil conversion on the diesel system," she replied haughtily. "The petroleum industry is horrible, and caring for the environment is important. Also, I get my used grease from a Japanese restaurant. I guarantee they don't use it for cooking *french fries*."

"How admirable of you." His features didn't so much as twitch. "At any rate, it's in the garage—but I do insist on driving something a bit less appalling to Oakland tonight."

She raised an eyebrow. "*Not* the Maserati. While I'm sure you played fast and loose with the humans' minds when you went to retrieve it, that's still courting trouble."

"No, not the Maserati," he agreed. "There's also an Aston Martin, only slightly scratched after the last time my troublemaking vampire protégé got into a car chase with it."

She perked up at the mention of Nigellus' pet vampire. "Oh, you mean the pretty English one? I met him once when I was trying to track you down. How's he doing these days, anyway?"

"Fine, though not currently on speaking terms with me," he said. "Long story."

If she didn't feel so terrible right now, she might have pursued that further. "Hmm. Well, I daresay he'll come around. It's not as though you can't wait him out. So, Oakland, you said?"

He nodded. "By way of Stockton, yes. Would you care to freshen up here first? We should leave as soon as possible."

"All right," she agreed. "Assuming there's nothing immediate that needs doing when it comes to the current murder and mayhem, that is."

"There's no additional news regarding Alice Ramirez, no. Edward will monitor the situation and contact me if he needs to."

She shrugged agreement, since honestly, what they needed right now was a mental breakthrough in the case—some way to reconcile all of its seemingly conflicting parts. That could happen as easily on the road as it could while sitting here in Calaveras County. And in the event of a major break, such as the police finding Alice, Nigellus was a demon. He could teleport them back here in the blink of an eye.

"Fine," she said. "Though I'm afraid I'll need to borrow a shirt for the trip to my apartment in Stockton. The humans can be dreadfully stuffy about such things, you know."

As it turned out, Edward had cleaned and repaired her blouse while she was busy being blackout drunk. The bra was a total loss, but Neveah still remembered the nineteen sixties, and couldn't marshal much in the way of caring.

It felt more than a bit odd allowing Nigellus into her private space—not because there was anything all that unusual about her modest apartment, but simply because he was a demon. Even before her people had slammed the so-called pearly gates shut on the other realms, angels and demons hadn't really interacted much. At least, not outside of their occasional pointless and tiresome wars throughout prehistory.

Still, it would have been unnecessarily rude to ask him to stay in the car—another flashy sports model that probably cost twice as much as most human families earned in a year. He came up with her in the elevator and waited politely in her living room, while she went into the back to wash and change.

Every movement dragged, and every time she jostled the half-healed wound that had ripped through her chest, she winced. Shrugging into a high-necked sleeveless blue dress that covered the ugly scar in her flesh, she gave herself a final look in the mirror. Still pale and ghastly... or perhaps *ghostly* would be a better word.

She donned a pair of low-heeled ankle boots and stashed her ID, phone, and a bit of cash in a discreet garter purse strapped around her upper thigh. With the swishy knee-length skirt covering it, its presence wasn't obvious.

Possibly, she should have been pushier about finding out exactly where Nigellus was taking her, but she was finding it very difficult to devote much energy to the idea. There was a certain guilty comfort in allowing him to take control of the situation, while she did nothing more strenuous than go along for the ride. Whether he truly knew a place that might help her replenish her reserves was an open question, but the chances were certainly better than if she'd curled up alone in her apartment to lick her wounds... so to speak.

"Is this all right?" she asked, indicating her clothing as she returned to the living room.

"Perfect," he replied, without breaking expression. Idly, she wondered when the last time he'd smiled had been.

They drove the remaining two hours or so to Oakland in relative silence. Nigellus navigated them to a less than savory looking intersection, where a youngish human male was standing on the corner with a messenger bag over his shoulder and a folded map held in his hand. The demon pulled up to him and rolled down the passenger window.

The young man beamed at her. "Buy a map, pretty lady?" he asked, glancing past her to Nigellus and then away again quickly.

"How much?" Nigellus asked.

"F-fifty bucks," the youngster stammered.

Nigellus handed over a hundred-dollar bill. "Keep the change."

The human gingerly handed Neveah the map, as though he feared Nigellus might leap across the center console and strike at him like a snake.

She took it and gave him a wan smile in return.

Nigellus rolled up the window and drove on when the light changed. Neveah unfolded the map with a frown.

"I wasn't aware paper maps were still a thing," she said.

"Only for certain applications," he replied, completely deadpan. "Is there a route marked?"

Light from the streetlamps illuminated the folded paper in waves of sodium-yellow. "Yes, the destination appears to be a little way southwest of the Coliseum." she frowned. "What's down there except old warehouses?"

"Very little," he said cryptically, and took the first turning to head them in that direction.

Despite her growing skepticism, she guided him to the bright red star printed on the map. It was, in fact, a derelict warehouse… except the weed-choked parking lot behind the building was teeming with other cars.

Hundreds of them.

When Nigellus parked and turned off the engine, Neveah became aware of a faint pulsing through the soles of her feet—the feel of heavy bass just beyond the range of hearing.

She raised her eyebrows at him. "Have you brought me to an illegal rave? I didn't realize those were still happening."

"They are, though not on the same scale that was common twenty years ago."

She turned to look at the warehouse—innocently dark and uninteresting on the outside, with only the vibration of loud music escaping from inside giving it away.

"It's all very *early nineties*, don't you think?" she said.

"A mere blink of the eye to an immortal, surely," he retorted, and she wondered for an instant if that had been meant as a joke.

"Granted," she allowed, "but I'm not entirely certain why you believe this will help?"

The look he shot her was almost pitying. "I take it that even in the nineteen nineties, you weren't a part of this scene."

"Er… not really, no."

"Perhaps you should have been," he said, rather cryptically.

For lack of any better options, she hauled her aching body out of the car when he opened the door for her, and allowed herself to be escorted to an inconspicuous side entrance on his arm — mostly because she did, in fact, need the support. Nigellus presented the map to a burly human man standing outside. He looked it over, looked *them* over, and nodded them inside with a jerk of his chin.

As soon as the door opened, Neveah was hit by a wave of… *something*. Empathy and fellow feeling and, yes — *love*. She breathed in sharply, barely aware of the pain in her chest beneath the unexpected flood of euphoric emotions.

Electronic dance music pulsed through the echoing space. Laser lights illuminated hundreds of heaving bodies in sharp, geometric bursts. A fog machine spewed white vapor across the dance floor.

The people here — they were so *happy*.

Neveah clutched at her demon companion's arm, her body already swaying to the visceral, pounding beat.

"What… what *is* this?" she asked, having to shout to be heard over the music.

"Human vice at its finest," Nigellus said dryly. "Thanks to the amount of chemical assistance floating around this place, I would expect you'll be able to attract a decent amount of platonic love without expending more energy than you gain from it."

She stared at him, open-mouthed and lost for words.

An attractive woman in bohemian clothing approached them before Neveah could untangle her tongue.

"Care to enhance your evening?" she asked. "Twenty dollars a tablet for E. Ten dollars a bottle for poppers."

Neveah watched in something of a daze as negotiations commenced and money changed hands. The woman disappeared into the crowd without a backward glance. Nigellus lifted a small green pill to his mouth and rolled it around on his tongue for a long moment.

"Reasonably pure," he declared. "Here. Take these."

"MDMA?" she asked.

"You might as well be on the same wavelength as the people you're going to be drawing from," he replied. "Also, there's the added pleasure I'm taking from the prospect of corrupting an angel."

She scowled at him and dry-swallowed the two pills he handed her without breaking eye contact.

"I believe the preferred method is to allow those to dissolve under your tongue," he said mildly.

"Too late. Have you been buying into Fae religious propaganda from the last war?" she asked, still having to speak loudly to make her words heard. "I already drank an entire bottle of your whiskey, you know."

"And that was also delicious to watch—although I could have wished for different circumstances."

She wrinkled her nose at him. "You and me both."

During the war, it had made tactical sense for the Fae on Earth to leverage their natural gifts by positioning themselves as angelic beings in the Abrahamic religious tradition. Neveah's people had interbred with the Fair Folk many thousands of years ago, introducing some of the magical traits common to the Fae today—most notably, the ability to manipulate human minds by engendering a form of adoration similar to what angels could elicit.

The angels—well, all of them except for her—had already abandoned the field of battle by the time it occurred to the Fae to impersonate them, in order to control large numbers of humans via the means of propaganda.

Since the Fae were genuinely a fussy race when it came to vice, they'd played up that aspect of the folklore. Angels were virtuous and pure. Demons were vile and evil and dangerous. Ultimately, that hadn't been the gambit that won the war for them—the winning strategy had been the destruction of most of Hell's vampire army in a single, devastating blow with an experimental magic weapon. But the Fae propaganda campaign had certainly put the demons on the back foot when it came to their interactions with humans on Earth.

Despite rumors to the contrary, Neveah's people weren't *fussy*. An awful lot of them were honestly pretty bloodthirsty... and a somewhat smaller subset was prone to siring half-breeds with the other, weaker races. As much as it pained her to admit it, they'd probably done the other realms a favor by self-isolating.

Meanwhile, Neveah was stuck here on Earth, and she had been for a *very* long time. She'd gone through periods of seeking out vice, but it had always felt hollow. In a life so long, a sense of meaning was difficult to come by... but she'd never found it at the bottom of a bottle or in the bed of a random human. Maybe she was only going through the motions these days—yet she could still find flashes of fulfillment in putting together the puzzle pieces of a really good news story.

And she would try to do that with the current tangle of confusing and contradictory clues. *Tomorrow*.

Right now, happiness and the humans' generalized *agape* love buffeted her from all sides. The music throbbed through veins left cold and sluggish by her damaged heart. Multicolored lights cut through the hazy atmosphere like living art, pulsing in time to the beat.

"Vice? I'll show you *vice*, demon," she called, and danced deeper into the crowd.

NINE

The angel swayed to the music, moving through the pulsing crowd exactly like the mythical creature she was. Nigellus could tell when the double dose of ecstasy overcame her weakened metabolism — could practically see the swirling waves of love bouncing back and forth between her and the groups of human partygoers that slid in and out of her orbit.

Considering the overwhelming noise and flashing lights, the venue was oddly relaxing, in the way that places Fae would avoid like the plague generally were for a demon living on Earth. There was a reason his kind tended to stick to bastions of vice, when they stayed on Earth at all.

Atlantic City. Vegas. Monte Carlo. New Orleans.

Nigellus shadowed the angel, keeping an eye on her despite the fact that it was almost certainly a foolhardy and unnecessary precaution. She was already immortal, and strengthening visibly beneath the drug-fueled onslaught of human empathy and adoration. But seeing her translucent skin earlier, along with the pain lurking behind her pellucid summer-sky eyes, had been... disconcerting.

Nigellus occasionally had cause to drain his reserves to nearly nothing, in the pursuit of a necessary and worthy goal. But for him, recharging was merely a matter of absorbing the energy inherent in time's turning. Or—though it was an increasingly rare occurrence since the treaty with the Fae had been struck—by reaping and absorbing the power contained in a human soul he'd bound.

The idea of having no access to energy for replenishment was a deeply disturbing one. By rights, he shouldn't care about the fate of the last angel on Earth. He'd met angels on the battlefield during the various and ultimately futile struggles between the two genuinely immortal races. They were vicious fighters—as, of course, were demons.

But even so, to withhold assistance from someone who had done him no harm, when he had the power to help her? That would have been needlessly cruel. And he hadn't been lying earlier. After her disturbingly successful attempt to bend his mind to her will, he was taking decided pleasure in the idea of, if not corrupting her, then at least bringing her further down to Earth… so to speak.

As she swayed and smiled her way through the packed dance floor, stopping to hug and kiss strangers as though they were long-lost friends, it was surprisingly difficult not to let his thoughts wander to what-ifs and might-have-beens.

What if Edward hadn't arrived at a critical moment to distract him, and he'd taken the angel against his living room wall? He'd seen the dizzy expression of shocked pleasure on her face. When it came to corrupting an angel, there were few more direct methods. Had she dallied with humans before — or with Fae, for that matter — during her long exile?

And, by Hell, why was he thinking like this? Her influence must still be lurking in his head.

The illegal rave would continue until dawn. He settled into the atmosphere of human decadence, almost regretting that none of the drugs available in the venue would have any appreciable effect on his metabolism.

Neveah danced, and as the hours slipped by, the terrible translucent quality of her body faded as she gained solidity and vibrancy. When she eventually wandered back to him and stumbled against his chest, laughing and drunk on human love, he steadied her and tried to remember what that sort of unselfconscious happiness actually felt like.

"You're brilliant," she called, over the pounding electronic beat. "This is brilliant! I want to do this every night!"

"I'm afraid these events don't happen every night," he said dryly. "How's your injury faring?"

She pressed a hand between her breasts, still smiling an angelically brilliant grin.

"All fixed! I feel—" She sighed and melted against his body, pliant. "—absolutely *wonderful*. Can we go get breakfast somewhere, please?"

<hr>

He took her to the nearest greasy spoon diner, which was apparently a popular destination for refugees from the rave. The sky in the east was just beginning to lighten from blue-black to navy, visible through the large window next to their booth.

Neveah tore into a plate of pancakes covered in syrup, whipped cream, and strawberries as though she hadn't eaten in an age. Nigellus sipped strong, black coffee that had less similarity to bilgewater than one might have expected from such a place.

"Tell me something," the angel said, pointing at him with a forkful of food.

He quirked an eyebrow in an invitation for her to continue.

"Why did you work so hard to avoid me for such a long time?" The fork, laden with pancake and syrup, disappeared between her full lips.

"Simple enough," he replied. "I realized immediately that there was something unusual about you, but I'd assumed you were a human with natural magic. Given the treaty provision regarding demonic interference with humans, it would have been reckless to interact with you any more than absolutely necessary."

She appeared to weigh that for a long moment as she chewed and swallowed.

"Fair enough," she allowed. "You don't seem too worried about all the recent interference with the police and the morgue staff at the hospital, though."

He chose his words with care. "I am cognizant of a great number of potential pitfalls related to the current situation. But *worrying* about any of them isn't useful."

The angel set down her knife and fork to regard him. "The whole thing's kind of spiraling out of control, don't you think? Alice is a loose thread, and every time we pull on it, the tangle only gets worse."

Nigellus was painfully aware of that fact.

"Is this really what you want to discuss right now?" he asked.

She sighed and pulled a plate of bacon, eggs, and hash browns toward her. "No, it very much isn't." Her face went dreamy again, radiant in its unearthly beauty. "How did you know to take me to that rave? I never realized humans could bond emotionally in big groups like that. It was lovely."

"MDMA is an interesting empathogenic chemical, at least when it comes to human physiology," he said. "Not always physically safe for them, of course—but still a fascinating study in psychosocial effects. And as far as how I got the idea, Ransley Thorpe's lover is a hybrid succubus. She often feeds from the lust of groups of humans who congregate in sex clubs. The emotion is different, but the principal is similar."

A smile tugged at one corner of Neveah's mouth. "Ah. Your pretty English vampire protégé again? Yes, I met his part-demon paramour. I don't think she liked me very much."

"Hmm. Were you asking her intrusive questions at the time?" Nigellus asked.

"Probably," she admitted. "I'm glad that your little vampire family is growing, you know. It would have been awful if the Fae had managed to wipe them out entirely."

The subject of vampires was not one Nigellus intended to venture into any further than that. The Fae had sacrificed their most powerful magical practitioners when they set off the weapon that destroyed the demons' army of the night in a single stroke. Nigellus—spymaster that he was—barely had enough warning to whisk Ransley Thorpe to safety in Hell before the cataclysm.

The existence of even one vampire meant the possibility to rebuild the vampire race in the future remained... but it had taken a terrible emotional toll on that last survivor. Ransley had never truly forgiven Nigellus for saving him, and had resisted turning other vampires for centuries. Only after he'd fallen in love, having no other choice to save the lives of those closest to him, had he relented. The entire vampire population now stood at three individuals—Ransley, his part-demon lover Zorah, and Zorah's grandfather, Guthrie Leonides.

Even now, Hell's Council had need of the vampires' blood for reasons of their own. But aside from the bare minimum of interaction necessary to fulfill that obligation, none of the three vampires cared to exchange words with Nigellus, or with any other demon.

"Yes," Nigellus agreed blandly. "I'm glad as well. It would have been a terrible waste."

Neveah ate slightly more than half of her second plate before flopping back in the booth with a heartfelt groan. "Oh, that was good." She nodded at the uneaten food. "Do you want any of this? I'm afraid I'm stuffed."

"No thank you," he replied. "Though I'm happy to add gluttony to the list of the night's deadly sins."

She snorted at him. "What—along with sloth? That makes two, and I was only slothful because I was recovering from a bullet wound. It hardly counts."

"You're forgetting lust," he pointed out dryly, even though it was probably ill advised.

A faint blush stained her cheekbones. "Ah. Yes. I really am sorry about that."

"Are you, though?" he asked.

The blush grew deeper. "Well, to be fair, you started it."

Which… true. And if Edward hadn't walked in, he probably would have finished it. The fact that she hadn't seemed averse to the prospect wasn't something he should be thinking about too much.

He'd assumed her to be human, and he'd treated her as such. It turned out she was well able to defend herself, and that miscalculation was on him, not her.

"You know, you were right earlier," he said conversationally. "You really aren't a very good angel."

She scrunched up her nose at him, and he tried very hard not to find it charming.

He drove east as the sun rose over neatly parceled California farmland. Much of it was planted in orchards, almond and walnut trees spaced out at precisely measured intervals. Fields of vegetables and occasional stretches of more natural looking trees broke up the monotony.

The angel gazed out at the profusion of orange, pink, and lavender coloring the dawn sky, so relaxed and sated that she looked as though she'd been poured into the car's passenger seat rather than sitting on it. The convertible's top was down. The breeze teased strands of platinum hair free from the messy bun she'd twisted it into, held precariously in place with a pen she'd borrowed from him.

"The human realm can be a truly lovely place," she said, over the roar of engine and wind. "And yet, I do miss my home."

Her tone sounded wistful.

Nigellus contemplated the idea of going millennia without seeing Hell's familiar, desolate beauty.

"What is it like?" he asked. "Heaven, I mean."

She seemed to ponder the question for a few moments.

"Idyllic. Uncomplicated." She hesitated. "Occasionally boring."

"That, at least, isn't generally an issue on Earth," he offered.

"No." The word emerged on the back of a sigh. "Well… yes and no. I suppose it depends how closely one pays attention."

Personally, Nigellus could have done with a little more boredom over the past few years. Between the drama surrounding Ransley and Zorah, and the increasing political instability in the Fae realm, he'd had quite enough excitement recently — even before receiving Baalazar's unwelcome news about the escaped prisoner.

They stopped in Stockton again so Neveah could pack an overnight bag, and afterward, they continued on to Vallecito, since it was closer to the center of the action. Edward greeted them when they arrived at the winery house.

"Ah, good. You're back," he said. "I need to take the car to Columbia College in hopes of speaking to some of Alice's professors." He gave Neveah an approving once-over. "You're certainly looking much better, Miss."

Neveah offered Edward a blinding smile — one with more angelic force behind it than she'd probably intended, because his servant blinked and visibly stopped himself from taking a startled step back.

"Yes, much," she agreed. "It was *lovely.*"

She still sounded drunk, and Edward shot Nigellus a concerned glance that clearly conveyed, *are you going to be able to handle this?*

"Carry on, Edward," Nigellus told him. "I need to update the Council on recent developments."

"Right you are, sir," said his servant, and bustled off to pursue his leads at the college.

Nigellus eyed his guest, whose expression still held a hint of a blissed-out smile. "Do please make yourself at home while I'm out — and I say that only because you won't find anything of interest in this house, should you decide to go snooping."

She donned an air of injured innocence, pressing a hand over her healed heart—eyes wide and guileless. "Would I?" she asked.

"I watched you crack a safe in less than two minutes yesterday," he reminded her. "At any rate, there's a swimming pool in the back, and a well-stocked entertainment room downstairs. I shouldn't be long."

Her teasing expression sobered. "Are you going to tell the Council about me?"

He opened his mouth to reply, and hesitated. "I... hadn't really considered the matter. Would you prefer I didn't?"

She arched an eyebrow. "On the contrary. Of all the sentients in the multiverse, I suspect the demons are best placed to offer useful insight into my unfortunate Heaven sitch. That's why I've been trying to chase *you* down, after all."

A sense of disquiet pricked at him. "I'm not entirely certain you should ascribe noble motives to demons collectively. While the Council would approach the situation from the perspective of what's best for political stability, there are a number of individuals in Hell who might seek to exploit your presence on Earth for their own gain."

She gave him an airy wave. "Well, I leave it to your judgment, then. We can talk about it when my head doesn't feel like it's stuffed with cotton candy and floating through the clouds."

"Probably for the best," he agreed, and slipped out of corporeal existence without further discussion, reappearing in the darkness on the human side of the gate to Hell.

He entered the familiar passage between realms, nodding to the guards stationed on the other side. "Has Baalazar left any messages for me?" he asked.

"He says to come immediately if you have anything to report," said the one called Melek — a burly demon of fate from the third rank.

"Thank you," Nigellus told him.

There was no telling whether Baalazar would be in his own chambers or in the middle of an important Council meeting. Nigellus tugged his shirt cuffs straight and reached inward, following the invisible trail of the blood he'd given Baalazar earlier.

The imp was, in fact, alone in his quarters — part of the vast network of dwelling and communal spaces carved into the living rock of Hell's massive sandstone cliffs.

"You have news?" he asked without preamble, and Nigellus launched into a synopsis of the situation as it currently stood. He glossed over Neveah's presence, on the basis that the current state of affairs didn't need complicating further.

Baalazar seemed relieved to hear that the prisoner's body had been destroyed, and skeptical of the need to pursue the investigation of Alice Ramirez... until Nigellus got to the part about the salt-packed bullet. At that, the imp's face went as stony as one of the granite gargoyles he superficially resembled.

"Could this young woman be a Fae operative?" he asked. "How else would she know how to set a trap for a demon?"

Nigellus spread his hands. "It's certainly one possibility. And if that's the case, it would be prudent to find her before she's able to report back to her Fae masters about the dead Seelie."

Baalazar frowned. "Yes… that could be disastrous, depending on how much she knows."

"Edward has gone to investigate the institution of higher learning where she was enrolled," Nigellus assured him. "With luck, someone there will have some insight into where she might have run."

"With *luck*, she drove off a cliff and this whole disastrous mess will be over," Baalazar muttered. He sighed. "But, luck doesn't usually work like that, as you know better than most."

"Indeed," Nigellus agreed. "I should be getting back now. But first, has Leyak recovered enough to explain himself?"

Baalazar shook his head in obvious irritation. "Not yet, the fool. I'll keep you posted with any developments on that end."

"Thank you, old friend," Nigellus told him, and took his leave.

Though it was not the most efficient use of his time, he walked back toward the gate rather than teleporting directly there. The angel's talk of missing Heaven had stirred something in him, and he took a few moments to appreciate the stark, desolate beauty of his original home.

The sun shone down mercilessly from an orange-red sky, illuminating the twisted rock formations with their multi-colored strata. In the valley below lay the settlement where a group of humans—sent to Hell by the Fae as a form of tithe—lived in a communal village of perhaps a thousand individuals.

That had been one of the few concessions by their Fae enemies at the end of the war—along with the continued survival of Ransley Thorpe, the last vampire not destroyed by the Fae weapon. The Fae seeded their own people among the humans as changelings, secretly replacing human babies with Fae ones. After the war, the demons demanded a tithe of one tenth of the infants in Dhuinne as a condition for a quick and peaceful resolution.

The Fae's assumption had been that the demand was intended as a way to control Dhuinne's population growth, limiting the future numbers of Hell's sworn enemies. No doubt they'd thought they were being clever by sending the human infants they'd stolen from Earth, rather than sending their own children. However, Fae were an inherently truthful race, and that put them at a disadvantage in contractual dealings with demons.

The small human settlement in Hell had a specific purpose in the ongoing political wrangling between the two races. Nigellus gazed down at the modest cottages with their thatched roofs, smoke from their cooking fires curling above the chimneys, and hoped that they weren't about to reach a point where those fragile human lives would be needed.

Shaking off the thought, he teleported the rest of the way to the gate. With a brief word of farewell to the guards, he slipped through to Earth… into the darkness and distant, eerie wailing of the Moaning Caverns. From there, he traveled directly to the winery house, his mind already returning to the puzzle awaiting him.

The place felt empty, so he went out the patio door in back to look for the angel. He stopped when he saw her—lying on a white towel next to the swimming pool. She was sunning herself, completely naked, the rays illuminating pale, radiant skin that no longer held so much as a hint of translucence. As though she'd felt his gaze on her, she turned eyes the same color as the aquamarine water on him.

And she smiled.

TEN

Nigellus was back, and Neveah still felt like she was floating on a cloud even though she was actually lying on a concrete pool deck.

She'd been contemplating something wicked during his absence, mostly because she was pretty sure the demon desperately needed to get out of his own head for a bit, almost as much as she needed to get *back* into her head. Unless Edward came up with some real gems of information from the college, they were stuck until one of them came up with a 'eureka' moment regarding whatever was really going on with Alice and her salt obsession.

"Hello," she said. "Any breakthroughs?"

"Sadly not," he replied.

He seemed to be watching her rather fixedly. She yawned and stretched, enjoying the way the sun's rays warmed her skin. His amber gaze never left her as she rose to her feet and padded toward him, pale hair draped over her breasts.

"Pity," she said. "Tell me, what would you say to carrying on where we left off yesterday, when Edward interrupted us so rudely? While we're waiting for inspiration to strike, I mean."

He raised a sharp eyebrow. "With or without mental manipulation being involved?"

She shrugged. "Your choice. But I think you need a distraction, and I *know* I do. Humans are too complicated for this sort of thing… and also a bit breakable. I'm sure you agree, given how shocked Edward seemed when he walked in."

"Still pursuing the seven deadly sins, then?" His tone could have cut glass.

"More religious references, really?" She walked into his space and took a deep, theatrical sniff. "Hmm… and hardly a hint of brimstone. Are you *sure* you went to Hell? You're not even singed."

He huffed air through his nose. "Your point is taken. But mine still stands. You should be careful what you ask for, angel."

"*Pride*," she announced, out of the blue. "How's that? I take pride in this body I crafted so long ago. That's another one of the sins, isn't it?"

"I believe that brings us to four, yes," he agreed.

"And you helped me fix it yesterday when it was broken," she said. "I like you, demon. You might play the untouchable immortal who's above it all—"

"Below it all, surely," he cut in. "Underworld, and all that."

She rolled her eyes at him.

"—but I don't think you're as unaffected by the people around you as you like to pretend."

It was a gamble, but she pressed her body against his, tilting her head up so she could watch his face as she hooked a finger in his unbuttoned collar and tugged. If she'd read him wrong, he could either take a step back, physically move her out of his space, or simply teleport away. If she'd guessed right—

His hand closed around the globe of her left buttock, pulling her lower body roughly against his. The sunny pool deck disappeared as he transported them through the ether, and they reappeared an instant later in the guest bedroom where she'd recovered the previous afternoon. He toppled her backward; she landed on the plush mattress of the generous queen-sized bed. She gazed up at him, and he stared down at her as though he were attempting to work out a complicated math problem.

The silence stretched for a heavy moment before he finally spoke.

"What you did to my mind yesterday—do it again."

She frowned, certain she'd misunderstood. "Sorry?"

"You heard me, angel." Very deliberately, he undid one onyx cufflink, and then the other, tossing them onto the bedside table. "Manipulate my mind again. See what it gets you."

A flutter in her stomach set butterflies dancing. "Are you sure?" she asked.

"I don't generally speak before I'm sure of things," he replied, and started on the buttons of his shirt.

She blinked, rearranging the current situation in her mind, and gave a small shrug. As kinks went, it wasn't the strangest she'd ever come across... assuming that's what was actually happening here.

"Well, in that case..." A small smile tugged at her mouth. "Look into my eyes, O Mighty Demon."

Love me, she thought. *Adore me. Worship me, because I am an angel.*

As before, the light behind his eyes... wasn't adoration. It *certainly* wasn't worship. Something low in Neveah's belly tightened at the memory of a commanding hand around her throat and a hard-muscled thigh between her own.

This time, she hadn't taken him by surprise, and he wasn't out of control. Orange flame kindled behind the black of his pupils, but he continued removing his clothes with steady deliberation, until he was as naked as she was. She watched, wide-eyed, taking in the appearance of the tattoos covering the skin of his right shoulder and arm.

She'd already seen the three crosses peeking above his unbuttoned collar, but that was just the tip of an artistic piece that stretched down the right side of his body. Below the crosses, an earthly landscape gave way to billowing smoke. Beneath the smoke stretched the biblical Hell, complete with winged demons circling his bicep and forearm, locked in battle.

The human guise they decorated was also a work of the shapeshifter's art, every bit as much as her own body was. He was tall... well muscled without being bulky, and he held himself with a natural-born fighter's poise. In that instant, she had a crazy desire to see him wield his stolen angelic sword in battle... and an even crazier desire to be his opponent in her true angelic form. To see if she could take it back from him.

That part of her warrior past was long gone, though. She still had the edge over him in a battle of mind against mind—at least with the element of surprise. But he could dominate her weakened human form physically without even breaking a sweat. This fact was demonstrated rather neatly when he stalked onto the bed on all fours, his body caging hers as he covered her.

He stretched her arms above her head one at a time, holding both wrists tightly in the grip of one long-fingered hand.

"Is this what you wanted, angel?" His voice was a low rumble. "Is this how you prefer to fall?"

She couldn't stop her full-body twitch in response to that particular turn of phrase.

"Too late for that," she whispered. "I've already fallen."

The unpleasant moment was forgotten the instant his hips rolled against hers. A gasp escaped her, as the same shuddering, tingling sensation she remembered from before flared along the length of her spine. She arched, chasing the feeling. He pushed her legs apart with his, leaving her splayed beneath his body like a butterfly pinned to a board.

His hard length stroked along her folds, and she bucked, already overwhelmed by the sheer physicality of what was happening between them.

"Sing for me, angel," said the demon, and sheathed himself inside her body with a single, unforgiving thrust.

The high-pitched, uneven cry that escaped her control wasn't exactly musical. She wrapped her legs around his hips, trying to get *more*, and was rewarded by a slow thrust that she felt all the way from her scalp to her toes.

"Y-*yes*," she managed in a wavering voice, bucking into the maddeningly slow rhythm. Neveah stared up into eyes burning with hellfire, unable to look away.

"See what you do to me," Nigellus rumbled. His voice grew deeper, more resonant. His pitch-black rams' horns curled into existence, sprouting from the silver-gray hair that dusted his temples. The body pinning Neveah's grew in weight and bulk, the member inside her swelling and growing ridges that dragged against her sensitive flesh with every inexorable thrust. Talons brushed the delicate skin of her wrists where he restrained her. "Is this what you wanted, little angel?" he asked.

"Yes," she said again, feeling the pleasure he was forcing on her begin to coil tight at the base of her spine. "*Yes*, I want this. Give it to me!"

Leathery black wings burst into existence above her, blocking out the light. The arm that had been holding her down by the wrists let go in favor of sliding beneath her back. He twisted sideways on the bed, bringing her with him as though she weighed nothing, his massive wings giving a single hard flap for balance as he rolled onto his knees. She ended up straddling his thighs as he knelt on the bed, holding her upper body against the hard muscles of his chest as gravity pulled her onto the demon cock currently splitting her in two.

Her mouth opened, but no sound emerged as he rolled his hips, filling her again and again. His large, clawed hands spread over her shoulder blades. His fingers flexed through more than three dimensions, reaching into a place that had been cut off and out of her grasp for years.

Neveah's wings burst into physicality with a sharp snap of white feathers cutting through air. She whimpered and came hard around him, her flesh pulsing and milking his as her wings fluttered weakly.

His movements inside her slowed as she came down from the shattering climax. She rolled her shoulders, folding first one wing and then the other so they nestled against her back. His larger, leathery wings mantled around her, enfolding her against him in a dark cocoon. She lay limp against him, heat and shivery pleasure radiating outward as his slow thrusts continued.

"What did you do?" she murmured in a daze, feeling her feathers brush against the warm expanse of the bat-like wings surrounding hers.

Her only answer was a low growl. Nigellus buried sharp teeth in her shoulder and stilled, his abdominal muscles jerking as he spilled into her. Another aftershock spasmed through her body in response, leaving her weak and trembling in his embrace.

When they were both spent, Nigellus lifted her off of his cock and tipped her carefully backward onto the mattress, mindful of her folded wings. He leaned over her, looking down at her with eyes full of hellfire, one arm braced beside her head. His physical bulk melted back into the form of a tall, well-muscled human male, hornless and wingless.

He had that expression again—that of a mathematician confronted with a knotty equation that didn't quite make sense. As though *she* were the complicated one… *honestly*. She had to resist the urge to huff at him in annoyance as she basked in the afterglow.

His eyes faded back to the amber color of top-shelf bourbon.

"Do your wings still itch?" he asked, as though he hadn't just had his teeth buried in her shoulder and his cock buried in her passage.

She gave an experimental wriggle.

"Yes. They do," she decided. "I must look a sight—the feathers haven't been preened in decades." With an awkward, out-of-practice shuffle, she rolled onto her side and got both wings behind her, hanging off the edge of the bed and giving him space to lie down facing her. His human-colored eyes never left her, and a crease of concentration marred his forehead.

"Tell me something," she asked, to fill the silence. "Why did you want me to influence your mind again?"

He rolled onto an elbow, looking down at her as he chose his words with evident care.

"Lust," he said eventually. "That's the province of incubi and succubi, not demons of fate. For most demons, sex is a transaction. Lust is a novelty… and in a life as long as ours, novelties are rare."

"That's painfully true," she agreed, thinking of the endless years of boredom and tedium in a life that spanned eons. She reached behind herself, running her fingertips through tangled and matted feathers as best she could.

"My turn," he said. "Why ask to be defiled by a demon?"

He looked genuinely curious.

Her half-smile was a little bit wistful… a little bit bitter. "You made me feel something. Not just with the sex, but also last night at the rave. I don't usually feel things, these last few centuries. I wanted to make sure I still could."

The look of understanding he gave her was somehow both terrible and wonderful at the same time.

ELEVEN

"Well, I suppose this was inevitable." Edward stood in the open door of the guest bedroom, with the air of a man who would have appreciated a bit more warning before walking in on two supernatural creatures lounging in post-coital lassitude on the bed.

Neveah smiled radiantly at him. "Hello! My wings are back, look!"

The elderly servant's gaze shifted to them as she gave them an experimental flutter. "Indeed, Miss. Er… congratulations?"

Nigellus sighed. "Did you learn anything useful at the college, Edward?" He swung his legs over the edge of the mattress and reached for his discarded trousers.

Edward averted his eyes politely. "I suppose it depends on your definition of useful, sir. Everyone I managed to speak to seemed eager to tell me what a wonderful young woman Alice was, and how she'd never shown so much as a hint of trouble. Average student, well liked by both students and professors, no known issues at home, and so forth."

"Hmm." Neveah scooted around and rolled onto her front, hugging a pillow. "To be fair, I suppose if she is a Fae operative, one wouldn't expect any obvious red flags in her daily life."

"True enough, Miss," Edward agreed, though he still looked troubled.

"None of which goes any way toward explaining her connection to the dead Fae prisoner," Nigellus said.

He was buttoning up his shirt now, and Neveah took a moment to regret that they had more important things to do than lounge in bed all day.

"So, what now?" she asked. "It feels as though we're at something of a dead end here."

Nigellus paused in doing up his cufflinks. "I need to see the guard, Leyak. Something occurred to me just now, relating to his slow recovery. I also need to get a message to a contact who can often be difficult to reach."

Neveah frowned, running over what she knew of the dismembered demon guard. "The missing salt pellets," she realized. "You think part of his body is encased in salt, and that's why he's not able to recall it and heal enough to speak?"

"It might explain a couple of things, yes," Nigellus agreed.

"While opening fresh questions regarding Alice's involvement in all of this," Edward added.

"Doesn't it just," Neveah mused, tapping her lower lip thoughtfully. "I need to think about that for a bit. There's something circling at the back of my mind, but I can't quite..." She trailed off and shook her head. "Anyway, while I'm thinking, I want to see about getting these old things cleaned up a bit before I put them away." She gave her wings another experimental flap.

"They do appear a bit worse for wear, Miss," Edward said delicately. "No offense intended."

"None taken," she told him. "I'm not entirely sure I'll be able to manifest them again once they're hidden. If that's the case, I'd at least like them to be clean and properly groomed first."

Edward nodded. "Understandable, Miss. There's an outdoor shower by the pool. I'll get you a towel to wear, and there should be some Dawn detergent in the kitchen. Stay right there; it will just take a moment."

———◆———

Nigellus excused himself to go visit the injured demon guard without offering much in the way of sentimentality… not that Neveah would have expected it of him. They'd connected, in the way of two lonely immortals who understood the challenges that came from an extremely long life… but immortals also understood better than most sentients that there was time for all things.

To everything there is a season, etcetera, etcetera. And right now, it was time to figure out what in heaven's name was going on with Alice Ramirez.

In Neveah's case, she hoped to let her mind accomplish this in the background while she got her poor wings back into some kind of decent shape. She'd always done her best thinking while distracted by the mundane. It was the angelic equivalent of a human's three a.m. revelation, she supposed.

Edward was at least a pleasant and interesting companion, especially for a human.

The open-air shower was intended for rinsing off before and after using the swimming pool, but it was also useful for anyone with a fifteen-foot wingspan.

"Will my nudity offend you?" Neveah asked.

"I've served a demon for centuries, Miss," Edward replied wryly. "Recent events aside, I daresay I'm fairly unshockable at this point. And in all honesty, bosoms and curves were never much of a draw for me, even as a young man."

"Oh, good," she said with some relief, and dropped her towel. "Because this really is going to be a two-person job."

In Heaven, wing grooming was an important social bonding exercise. It was one of many things she missed with a terrible, deep-seated ache of nostalgia. She turned on the shower and adjusted the temperature until it was pleasantly warm, but not hot. Meanwhile, Edward removed his sober black suit jacket and rolled up his sleeves.

Between them, they soaped and rinsed the feathers of first one wing, and then the other. The weight of the large, wet limbs was startling after so long. It was disconcerting to think that her flight muscles might have atrophied over the decades. She set the unpleasant thought aside.

"Stand back," she warned, before giving them a good shake to dislodge as much of the water as possible. It went flying in a fine spray, like a long-haired dog shaking itself off after a bath.

Edward helped her blot up more of the moisture with towels, being careful not to bend the feather vanes against the direction of growth. When that was done, she wrapped a fresh towel around her torso as a nod to human propriety and settled onto one of the sun loungers scattered around the pool deck.

"It's just a matter of preening the feathers into position as they dry, now," she said, extending her left wing forward and examining the primaries.

Edward watched her movements as she dragged her fingers through the coverts, aligning the small feathers and smoothing the barbs into place. After a few minutes, he started on the right wing with careful, precise movements.

She hummed in contentment, feeling oddly at peace despite the series of slow-rolling crises piling up in the background. The feeling of hands not her own sliding through feathers and down sent a pleasant tingling along her shoulders and spine. It made her feel... *angelic*. Properly so.

"Why don't you tell me a bit about yourself?" she suggested, after they'd been working for some time. "I've been wanting to chat with you about the wards on this place. They're rather impressive, especially for a human practitioner. Where did you learn wardsmithing like that?"

"From demons, of course," Edward replied, sounding mildly amused. His gnarled fingers didn't slow in their deft movements. "Beyond that, it's mostly a matter of having time to practice and perfect the art. I'm certain you of all people can appreciate that."

"True," she agreed. "So, your demon bond with Nigellus predates the Fae treaty, I take it?"

It would have to, she assumed, since contracting for a human's soul was a blatant example of interference on Earth. It might still happen on occasion, but no demon would flaunt it by making the bound party a literal servant—especially while living more or less openly on Earth.

"Oh, yes," Edward replied. "It predates the end of the war by quite a number of centuries, as it happens. I bartered my soul to the metaphorical devil in the Year of Our Lord, thirteen hundred and forty-six."

Neveah shot him a surprised glance. She guessed him to be perhaps three hundred years old—not more than twice that. "Goodness. Congratulations. I believe you have the honor of being the oldest human I've ever met."

He chuckled. "Thank you, I think."

There was a story here. If Neveah had been in 'investigative reporter' mode, her nose would have been twitching. As it was, she was still curious.

"May I ask what you bartered your soul for? If it's not too personal, that is. Also, where are you from? You've clearly scrubbed your original accent."

Edward gave a little huff. "I'm originally from Perthshire, in Scotland, though I've changed my accent several times. I've had to, because not even the most impenetrable of modern Glaswegians would be able to make heads or tails of a fourteenth century Scottish accent. As for what I bartered? Well... noble titles were rather more important back then than they are today. I tried to grasp one that wasn't mine to claim. In the end, I wasted half of my mortal lifetime on that foolish quest."

She raised an eyebrow. "And when he called in your soul-debt, Nigellus made you a servant? Interesting."

Though not, perhaps, as interesting as the fact that Nigellus had kept Edward around for the next six centuries, rather than reaping him for more power during the darkest depths of the Fae war.

Edward gave a little shrug. "I think it amused him, and these days, even I can appreciate the irony. I fear I'm better suited to this life than I ever was to my own."

Neveah pondered that for a moment.

"Are you happy?" she asked. "Because some might say that humans aren't designed for a lifetime spanning hundreds of years."

In his turn, Edward took some time to frame his response. "I am happy sometimes, yes. I'm also sad sometimes, and bored sometimes, and frightened sometimes. I'm even angry on rare occasions. In short, I may be an exceptionally *old* human, but I am still... *human*."

She digested his words.

"I envy you that."

Edward's fingers slowed in their movements through her feathers. "I suppose that's understandable. I've had something of a ringside seat to the immortal experience. It seems that as millennia stretch into eons, the passage of time does begin to wear on a soul. I hope never to reach that point of jadedness. But if I do…" He trailed off, his hands going still.

"Yes?" she asked curiously.

He shook his head briskly. "Ah—don't mind me. It's a silly thing to worry about."

Neveah frowned. "Is it?"

"It is," Edward said firmly. "My soul is no longer my own, but Nigellus has promised that my death will be in the time and manner of my choosing. Not many humans can say as much."

That was an extremely interesting tidbit. Neveah filed it away for future consideration. A soul contract with a demon was a knotty proposition for the mortal involved. The ways in which it benefited the demon in question were straightforward enough—that demon could reap the contracted party's soul for power at any time and across any distance.

The ways in which it benefited the other person were more complicated. A human who sold their soul generally did so for some sort of concrete benefit, as in the case of Edward and his coveted noble title. But as long as a demon wished for their acquisition to stay alive… they would.

No matter what.

Just as demons could draw out the energy contained in the human's soul—thereby killing them—they could also funnel energy to that human for the purpose of healing injuries, halting aging, and curing disease. Demons were immortal and vastly powerful. As long as Nigellus decided to keep Edward alive, then alive he would stay. *Indelibly.* And if he had also promised Edward the death of his choosing, that said something very important about how much the demon spymaster valued his human servant.

"That was very nice of him," she said.

"I suppose it was," Edward agreed. He tweaked the last few secondaries on her right wing into position and smoothed them down. "There, now. How's that?"

The California sun had dried her feathers as they'd worked. She gave a flutter, settling everything into place.

"*So* much better," she said in relief. "Thank you for helping. I can't begin to describe what a relief that is."

He smiled, the expression deepening the wrinkles at the corners of his eyes. "It was a pleasure, my dear. Grooming angel wings isn't the sort of experience one turns down when it's offered."

She flapped experimentally a few times, feeling the muscles pull and strain after such a long stretch of disuse. Then, she sighed. "I don't want to put them away, for fear I won't have the energy to manifest them again."

Edward's expression grew sympathetic. "I'm afraid the human world isn't designed with fifteen-foot wingspans in mind. But perhaps you could, er... repeat the activities that allowed you to regain access to them on a more regular basis?"

She considered the suggestion. "Do you mean the rave? Or the sex?" Either way, the idea held some merit.

Edward's cheeks pinked. "I meant the rave, assuming it was the free-floating love in the air that replenished your strength. Events like that aren't so terribly difficult to come by in this part of the world."

"Oh. Yes, you're probably right," she agreed. "And I apologize for shocking your sensibilities earlier. I take it your master doesn't usually indulge in the carnal arts?"

Edward lifted a bushy eyebrow, mildly reproving. "You'd have to ask that question of him, Miss. Not me."

"Of course. Forgive me. But regardless, I'll wager he doesn't indulge on Earth," she said, as understanding dawned. Edward would have assumed she was human when he walked in on them that first time. Nigellus might couple with other demons from time to time—a transactional exchange, as he'd described it. But he wouldn't openly flout the treaty by having sex with a human. "Well, again—I apologize. The first time was a bit of a miscalculation on my part." Honesty compelled her to add, "The second time was actually quite nice, though."

Edward's gaze slid over her wings, resplendent now in their pale glory. "It does appear to have been somewhat inspirational," he said, deadpan.

With a small snort of laughter, she rolled her shoulders briskly, banishing the appendages to the dimension where they slept when she wasn't using them. The temptation to immediately call them back was great, but if she didn't try, she couldn't fail. For now, she could pretend that they were once more available at her beck and call.

Neveah tugged the towel a bit more snugly around her body and glanced up to gauge the height of the sun. Disappointingly, no grand revelations regarding the mystery had occurred while she'd been relaxing.

"Right. Back to work, I suppose," she said. "I do hope Nigellus is able to get some useful information regarding Leyak. That aspect of the situation is truly a bit baffling."

"Indeed it is." Edward looked thoughtful, and a bit worried. "On the one hand, if Leyak had reaped the Seelie after her escape, that would explain her sudden death and the lack of visible injuries. But he was already down for the count by that point. With his skull in multiple pieces, he shouldn't have been conscious enough to manage it."

"And if he had still managed it somehow, that much of an energy boost should have kick-started his physical regeneration," Neveah added. "Ugh. The whole thing is a maddening maze of contradictions."

"And none of it explains Alice," Edward said. "That part is bothering me quite a bit, to be honest. I've spoken to the young woman on numerous occasions over the years, as I often have reason to visit the gate to Hell. Not that one person can ever truly know another's heart, but I would have sworn blind that she was exactly what she seemed—a very sweet and uncomplicated college student working a summer job for experience and pocket money."

Neveah thought back to the landlady's corpse, blood from her sliced throat decorating Alice's bathroom like grotesque modern art.

"We need a fresh set of eyes on this," she decided. "While Nigellus is pursuing the Leyak angle, I think it's time I renewed an old acquaintance who might have some useful insight."

TWELVE

Neveah had a strong suspicion that Nigellus wouldn't approve of her meeting with this particular contact regarding this particular matter. He might have even had a point about that. However, there were a limited number of people available who would be able to offer fresh insight into this mess, and neither she nor Nigellus seemed to be bursting with useful ideas.

For that reason, she excused herself from the demon's house before he returned from his latest meeting in Hell. Her car was in the garage as he'd said it would be, and after a final round of profuse thanks to Edward for his help with her wings, along with a promise to report back when she learned anything new, she headed off to send a message.

Reaching her friend the cat-sidhe was generally a complicated affair involving go-betweens and a fair amount of waiting. While she was kicking her heels, Neveah killed time by running through all the available news coverage of the Seelie's death, Alice's disappearance, and the landlady's murder.

Of the former, there wasn't much since Nigellus had brought his influence to bear in the cover-up. Of the latter, there was quite a bit. Alice still hadn't turned up anywhere, and was being described as a person of interest for the time being, rather than a suspect.

There was some speculation in opinion pieces that she might have been a victim of foul play rather than the perpetrator. Neveah had suffered a salt-packed bullet through the heart that argued rather strenuously against that interpretation. Of course, she also had a six-hundred-year-old demon-bound butler who seemed ready to stand as a character witness on the girl's behalf... and Edward struck Neveah as a competent judge of character.

When she finally received a return message from the sidhe, it was a relief. Neveah arrived at their usual meeting place—a rock formation in Mt. Diablo State Park that the humans rather ironically called the Devil's Pulpit. The place was a reasonably short drive from Stockton, and accessible via a fire road with only a minimal amount of hiking involved.

It was also on a ley line, meaning a Fae could travel there magically without expending the sort of energy required to cast a portal from halfway across the world.

A black cat sat at the base of the distinctive, thirty-foot tall metamorphic stone outcrop, idly washing its paw. The area was blessedly free of tourists today, meaning there were no witnesses other than Neveah to see the animal's body twist and morph into a short humanoid figure with black hair and large, forest-colored eyes.

The sidhe were a race of genderless, shape-shifting proto-Fae who predated the Seelie and Unseelie on Dhuinne. They were vanishingly rare now, and largely reclusive — but still revered in Fae culture for their wisdom and magical prowess.

The cat-sidhe — an androgynous figure wearing buckskin and linen dyed in shades of green and tan — was somewhat childlike in voice and appearance... except for the eyes. Those huge green eyes had seen a lot, and the mind behind them was quick and wise.

Fae were not immortal in the same sense that angels and demons were. They had offspring. They grew old. They died, eventually. They just did all of those things exceptionally slowly, and the sidhe were longer-lived than most.

Neveah didn't know exactly how old the cat-sidhe was, and she had no intention of asking. They'd met after the war, when everything was in upheaval and it seemed as though all the rules had changed. For a long time, the sidhe had been the only being in the three realms who knew Neveah was an angel.

They'd found a certain understanding with each other — an angel locked out of Heaven, and a Fae who disagreed with many aspects of the Court's decisions regarding both the war and the uneasy peace that came afterward. Neveah had absolute faith that the sidhe would always act in the interest of peace between the realms, rather than for the self-centered political interest of the Seelie and Unseelie.

"Hello, my friend," she greeted. "I'm afraid we have a potentially serious problem."

"Hello." The cat-sidhe sniffed the air delicately as Neveah came to a halt in front of them. "Is this problem demon-related, by any chance?"

Neveah resisted the irrational urge to sniff her armpits. "Good grief. You can *smell* him on me? *Really*? I've showered twice since then!"

The sidhe shrugged. "I can, yes. Ooh, was it the spymaster? It was, wasn't it? *Hmph*. I suppose something like this was inevitable."

Neveah stared at the little Fae, bewildered. "Why do people keep saying that to me?"

"Well, you *have* been stalking him for years," the cat-sidhe pointed out, reasonably enough. "And it appears you finally caught him. Did you get any useful answers to your questions about Heaven's gate?"

She sighed. "No. Instead, I got a dead Seelie warrior on Hell's doorstep, a missing human girl who sets salt-laced booby traps for demons, and the potential for a major inter-realm diplomatic incident if we can't figure out how those two things are related. So, would you like to try and help me keep everything from going *boom*?"

The sidhe's elfin brows drew together sharply. "I think maybe you should start from the beginning and tell me everything."

"Yes." The voice, dry as dust, came from behind Neveah. Her senses prickled, and she turned just in time to see Nigellus stroll around the side of the rock formation, impeccable in a dark two-piece suit. "I'd quite like to hear this as well."

"Hello, Nigellus," said the cat-sidhe. "Fancy meeting you here."

Neveah looked between them. "Wait. You two *know* each other?" She pinned the sidhe with an accusing look. "You never said."

The Fae gave her a quizzical tilt of the head. "True. But I also never said I didn't know him. Besides, you never asked."

Nigellus was also giving the sidhe a narrow look. "I'm equally surprised to find that you two are acquainted. Though perhaps I shouldn't be." He seemed to shake off his momentary surprise. "I suppose it's fortuitous, even though I've been reluctant to involve anyone from Dhuinne before now, no matter how discreetly."

The cat-sidhe sighed. "Well, this all sounds unpleasantly ominous. Someone tell me the story, please, so I know what sort of damage control we're discussing."

With a wary glance at the demon, Neveah filled the sidhe in on the escaped Fae prisoner, the dismembered guard, Alice's suspicious disappearance, Nigellus' wanton flambéing of the corpse in the morgue, and finally, the booby trap in Alice's abandoned apartment. When she was done, the cat-sidhe leveled a baleful look at Nigellus.

"I suppose you had to destroy the body," they said. "And you've still no idea of the Seelie's identity?"

"None," Nigellus said evenly. "I was rather hoping you would have some insight on the matter."

"Unfortunately not." Arms crossed, the sidhe paced restlessly back and forth. "You must already know how the Court would react to this story. An undeclared Fae prisoner in Hell, captured *after* the treaty went into effect?"

"She wasn't captured." Nigellus spoke without inflection. "And you also know how the Court would have reacted to a Seelie prisoner being returned to them after having been bound to a demon. They would have considered it the ultimate insult, and reopened hostilities there and then."

The sidhe huffed. "Yes, yes. It was an untenable situation, I'll grant you that much. And it probably would have been fine if you'd simply kept the cell door locked... since it's apparent she hasn't been missed before now. *Ugh*. What was that fool of a guard *thinking*?"

Nigellus shook his head. "It will be difficult to know the answer to that question until he's in a condition to talk."

"Yes," Neveah agreed. "Speaking of which, any news on that front?"

"In a manner of speaking," Nigellus replied. "It's his heart, apparently. It still hasn't even begun to regenerate."

A terrible, sinking feeling took up residence in Neveah's stomach as the puzzle pieces finally began to fall into place, one by one. "The bag of salt in Alice's apartment," she said.

The sidhe looked between them. "The Seelie cut out his heart and took it with her?"

Neveah pinched the bridge of her nose. "Yes, it seems likely. But it's even worse than that."

"You've realized something," Nigellus said. "Tell me what it is."

"You won't like it." She rubbed at the corners of her eyes and let her hand fall. "Okay. Bear with me for a minute, because actually, *neither* of you are going to like this. This Seelie was bound to Leyak when she escaped and overpowered him outside the gate, yes? There's no disputing that."

"No, there isn't," Nigellus agreed. "She could not have left Hell otherwise."

"Right," Neveah said. "So, look at the timeline. First, the Seelie allows Leyak to bind her soul, and then she uses him to escape. Once she's past the gate, she overpowers him somehow, hacks him into pieces to keep him out of the picture for a few hours, and takes his heart with her. Next, she exits the Moaning Caverns, confronts Alice in the gift shop, and forces her into the restroom for privacy."

The demon sucked in a sharp breath. "After which, the prisoner's body is found, but she's no longer in possession of Leyak's heart, and Ms. Ramirez is missing."

The cat-sidhe's gaze bounced between them as they spoke.

Neveah took up the thread. "And then Alice — a perfectly normal human college student by all accounts — goes home, sets up a booby trap for demons, packs the heart in salt pellets, and brutally murders her elderly landlady before skipping town."

"You think the Seelie prisoner mentally influenced Alice Ramirez to do her bidding before she died," Nigellus said.

The sinking feeling in Neveah's gut grew worse. "No. I think the Seelie prisoner physically possessed Alice, melding their souls into one being as a way to escape the soul-bond she'd forged with Leyak. I think your prisoner hijacked a human and is wearing her body like an off-the-rack suit." She met the sidhe's green gaze. "Is it possible?"

The sidhe looked deeply troubled. "It's conceivable. Human minds are weak and susceptible to Fae influence. A powerful enough practitioner might be able to effect a full transfer, if they were willing to commit a form a suicide to do so."

Neveah turned her attention to Nigellus. "And the soul-bond?"

The demon's features had settled into grim lines. "I'm not aware that such a thing has ever been tested. But if the Seelie's soul is now commingled with another's—"

"Then it's no longer the soul Leyak bargained for," Neveah finished. "The Seelie's body is dead and turned to ash. The soul is a hybrid, though still controlled by the Fae."

The sidhe started pacing again. "This is bad. This is *very bad*. If you are right about this, and the human manages to reach other Fae and convince them of the truth…"

"It will spark precisely the diplomatic incident that the Demon Council hoped to avoid," Nigellus finished.

The sidhe rounded on Nigellus. "You must find this human and confine her to Hell before she contacts the Fae. That is the only way to avoid a political crisis between Hell and Dhuinne."

"Wait, *what*?" Neveah said. "Hang on a minute. Alice is an innocent victim here."

Nigellus turned hard eyes on her. "An innocent victim controlled by a cold-blooded murderer—one dangerous enough to mentally overpower not only a human, but also a demon."

"But still a victim!" Neveah retorted, appalled.

The demon didn't back down. "Would you prefer her to be killed outright? Because I guarantee the Council will demand either one solution or the other."

Neveah whirled to the sidhe. "You *cannot* be in favor of this."

The cat-sidhe appeared deeply perturbed. "Dhuinne is undergoing political instability on a scale not seen in generations. The Wild Hunt escaped the Court's control last year and wiped out a significant number of the Unseelie members during its rampage across the realms. The Fae realm's magic is unbalanced, and while efforts are being made to correct that, things are at a delicate stage. The life of one human—"

"Is still a *life*!" Neveah said.

"You didn't see the devastation the Hunt caused," Nigellus said quietly. "Not only within Dhuinne, but also on Earth. It tore through the veil and devoured all living things in its path. I believe you were the one who expressed a desire not to see the human realm turned into 'a giant sheet of volcanic glass,' as you put it."

Neveah opened her mouth... only to close it again a moment later.

"I fear what could happen to the balance between realms if Dhuinne turns its current internal chaos outward with intent," the sidhe said quietly. "It was bad enough when the damage was only collateral."

"You're bartering human life," Neveah told them, appalled.

Nigellus raised an eyebrow, and Neveah realized how that must have sounded to a demon. His people had bartered in human lives for as long as the human race had existed. As for the Fae, most of them considered Earth's citizens as little more than cattle.

She had expected better of the cat-sidhe, though.

"There is one aspect of all this that still concerns me," the sidhe said.

"Only one?" Neveah shot back.

The sidhe didn't respond to that directly. "The demon's heart. Why carry around something so deeply incriminating? What is the benefit?"

"Perhaps to prevent Leyak from awakening?" Nigellus suggested. "If the angel's theory is correct, the soul-bond is no longer a concern. But the imp may still have important information to impart."

Neveah turned a flat stare on him. So, she was reduced to being merely 'the angel' again, was she?

"This Fae was stuck in Hell for a long time," she said. "Maybe she just wanted a trophy."

The cat-sidhe went perfectly still.

"Or," Neveah went on, "maybe she's bug-fuck crazy after being an amnesiac prisoner for almost two hundred years, and we should be concentrating on a way to perform a Fae exorcism instead of talking about murdering or incarcerating her victim!"

"Forgive me. I must return to Dhuinne now," the cat-sidhe said abruptly. "Please try to find and deal with this human before the rest of the Fae find out about her."

With that, the sidhe called up a flaming portal and stepped through it. The burning oval snapped shut the moment they disappeared through it.

THIRTEEN

The angel threw up her hands in frustration. "Great. Well, *that* was an amazing help."

Nigellus eyed her warily, attempting to gauge how much of an obstacle she might become if she truly set herself against the necessity of containing this compromised human.

"Your hypothesis about the soul-transfer is certainly a breakthrough, assuming it's true," he said.

She rounded on him, all righteous anger, and even now he felt himself respond to her in unexpected ways. It was still novel. It was not, however, very useful under the current circumstances.

Her blue eyes snapped at him. "How is it ethical to send a perfectly innocent human being to Hell, when it was the demons' fault that she was put in the path of danger in the first place?"

Nigellus spared a thought for the hundreds of human tithelings residing in Hell after being sent there by the Fae. "How is it ethical to risk a war across realms, when the prompt removal of a single person could prevent it, thereby saving countless lives?" he retorted.

Neveah stared at him, as though she were somehow surprised by his answer. As though she didn't know him at all. He pushed that last thought away as ridiculous. Of course she didn't know him, just as he didn't truly know her. It was foolishness to believe otherwise.

"A sentient, living creature is not disposable," she said. "A human being is not a means to an end, no matter how worthy or important you've convinced yourself that end might be."

He stared back, wondering how an immortal could possibly have existed throughout the rise of human history, and still believe such a thing.

"Everyone is ultimately a means to an end," he said slowly. "No matter how much we might wish it to be otherwise."

Her head moved back and forth in unconscious negation of his words. "Do you truly believe that? Because, I'm sorry, Nigellus—but what a sad and terrible universe that would be."

He took in her delicate features; her pale, white-gold hair like spun silk. "You didn't fight in the Fae war."

She frowned. "No, I didn't. What would have been the point? I've had more than enough of war."

He didn't say that perhaps an angel fighting alongside the demons' army might have tipped the balance in their favor. Perhaps her presence, back when her powers were less drained, might have somehow prevented the slaughter of the vampires or prevented the humans from falling under Fae control.

Instead, he repeated, "You didn't fight in the war. You haven't seen firsthand what the Fae are willing to do to protect what they consider their best interests. The life of Alice Ramirez holds no more value in their eyes than the life of a pig or a cow in the eyes of the humans. If I can capture her, she will be humanely treated in Hell. Perhaps, once she is safely contained, some method of extracting the Seelie prisoner's soul from hers can be devised."

The angel's burning gaze didn't waver. "I may not have fought in *that* war, but it doesn't mean I haven't fought in other wars. How do you think I learned to steer clear of them? The fact remains that you want to punish an innocent human who happened to be in the wrong place at the wrong time. And not just *one* human. How do you think her parents are going to react if she disappears without a trace, with no body and no explanation? Somehow, I don't think telling them *'Oh, she's fine, she's just being guarded by demons as a prisoner in Hell'* is going to be much of a comfort."

"This argument isn't useful," Nigellus said, because frankly, this argument was the *opposite* of useful. Time was of the essence if they wished to avert disaster.

Neveah's cupid's-bow lips pressed together. "Fine. How about *this* argument instead? My meeting with the cat-sidhe was intended to be private. You gate-crashed it. Why? And perhaps more importantly, how?"

The angel didn't need to know that Nigellus had sent his own message to the cat-sidhe earlier in the day, requesting a meeting to discuss this very situation. The little Fae had been an ally of long standing when it came to conducting sensitive, back-door negotiations with the Fae. However, the necessity of communicating discreetly across realms meant that such meetings could take a while to arrange. At least this current minor comedy of errors meant he'd saved a bit of time.

"Why did I come?" he replied. "Because I wished to relay the findings about Leyak's missing heart, and see if you'd found out anything useful in my absence." His eyes slid down her body without his conscious volition, and he dragged them back up. "As to the 'how,' it occurred to me that I would have left a small amount of my essence inside you when we had intercourse. It was easy enough to follow that trail, though I realize now it was presumptuous of me to do so."

Her gaze flew down to her own belly, and she stared at her body with a look of surprise that was almost comical. There was nothing amused in her expression when she looked up again, though. "Well, you can take your 'essence' back *right this instant*," she snapped.

He reached out with a thought and took back most of what he'd spilled inside her, but not all of it—aware that the subterfuge might come back to haunt him at some unspecified future date. If she was truly intent on setting herself against him, though, it would be useful to have a way to track her.

"I've taken it back," he said without inflection. "Now, I'm afraid I must ask you not to pursue this matter any further."

Her beautiful features hardened into marble stillness, a hint of the fearsome angelic host of old shining through. "Nigellus—please know that I mean it in the broadest of philosophical and meta-phorical terms when I say, *go to hell.*"

With that, she turned her back on him and stalked toward the road visible on the next ridge, where her ridiculous car was no doubt parked. Seething with frustration over very nearly every single aspect of the current situation, Nigellus wrenched his physical form through the ether and back to the winery house.

Edward looked up, startled by his sudden re-appearance. "Sir? Any luck?"

Nigellus waved him off in irritation. "There's been a development. The need to find Alice Ramirez has now become pressing."

Edward's bushy brows drew together. "You mean, it wasn't before?"

Impatiently, Nigellus filled his servant in regarding the angel's theory about the Seelie prisoner's death and subsequent possession of the human woman.

Edward closed his eyes briefly. "Oh, *blast it all.*"

"What?" Nigellus asked, wondering if there was some further implication he'd missed due to his current state of vexation.

"Well, it's *Alice*, isn't it?" Edward replied, rather cryptically. "The poor child. I knew something was off about the situation, what with the landlady's death and the booby trap, but this? It's *terrible.*"

"Sentimentality, Edward?" Nigellus asked, wondering if the angel's influence was catching somehow, like human flu.

The look Edward shot him was mildly reproving. "Did you never speak to the girl when you were passing through? She'd been working in the gift shop for some time, you realize."

"You know I didn't," Nigellus said with some impatience. "When I need to use the gate, I travel directly to it."

"Then you've missed out on making the acquaintance of a very sweet young woman with a quick mind and a kind soul," Edward said, the reproach in his tone doing nothing to improve Nigellus' mood.

When he didn't answer, Edward sighed. "Right. Never mind. So, how are we getting this Fae hijacker out of her, once we find her?"

"I have absolutely no idea," Nigellus said. "At the moment, I'm only concerned with capturing her and getting her safely into Hell. Preferably before she leaves a trail of dead bodies obvious enough to get the attention of the other Fae on Earth."

"Well, did you talk to Ms. Lane about it?" Edward asked. "She does seem to be a competent investigator, which makes her a good resource when it comes to finding someone who doesn't want to be found. Wasn't that what she went off to do yesterday?"

Nigellus' irritation ratcheted up another notch. "I spoke with her. We had words."

Edward blinked at him. "Words... about what?"

"The disposition of a single human whose capture could decide the fate of entire realms,"

Nigellus said. "I've asked her not to pursue the matter any further."

There was a heavy pause.

"I see," Edward replied, with the sort of blandness that meant he had opinions he knew Nigellus wouldn't appreciate. Apparently, the struggle to keep them to himself was too great, however. "Forgive me, but is it really a good idea to alienate an angel who can overpower your mind without breaking a sweat, sir?"

Nigellus unclenched his jaw with an effort. "Right now, it feels like an *excellent* idea. Enough about the angel. What options do we have when it comes to tracking a Fae-possessed human on the run? It may be time to call in some debts, if that's what it takes."

Edward blew out a breath. "Er... let me think for a minute. We could try tracking credit card transactions. Or rather, I could try that, while you go talk to Alice's parents and extract anything they might know about her friends, or about places she might have connections to."

"Very good," Nigellus said. "Get started right away. We may not have much in the way of time."

FOURTEEN

Neveah's righteous anger lasted for the entire trip back to Stockton. It wasn't entirely aimed at the demon—though he hadn't earned any points for marking her like a wandering pet with a GPS tracker on its collar. No, she was feeling less than angelically inclined toward the cat-sidhe as well. That meeting hadn't gone at all the way she'd hoped.

Some people might have been taken aback by her defense of the same human who'd made a spirited effort to discorporate her via a large-caliber bullet through the heart. That was the entire point, though. Neveah felt quite confident now that Alice was innocent when it came to all the terrible things happening around her over the past few days.

She recalled Edward's utter shock upon learning that Alice was somehow involved in the Seelie prisoner's death, and his insistence that she was nothing more complicated than a sweet-natured college student working a summer job for extra money. It was the idea that Alice might still be trapped in there, aware of what was happening, that roused Neveah's protective instincts. And logically, the human *must* still be present in her body, at least to some extent. Otherwise, the Seelie wouldn't have been able to slip out of her soul-bond with Leyak.

That trick only made sense if the two souls had truly commingled.

If her theory was correct—and Neveah was convinced there was no other way to explain all the facts—it meant that a young, innocent human had been forced into a front row seat for murder and mayhem, doomed to watch helplessly as her body committed horrible acts of violence. Alice would have known her landlady personally. Maybe they were friendly, or maybe they weren't. But either way, the cruelty inherent in that murder would have been nightmarish for someone not already inured to violence.

The Fae controlling Alice's body was undeniably dangerous. But Neveah was damned if she'd let that fact sentence the Seelie's innocent human hijacking victim to a lifetime of punishment.

Back at her modest apartment, Neveah scrolled through her phone contacts and hit the call button. The recipient picked up on the fourth ring.

"Hello?"

"Hello, Paul. It's Nev," she said. "I need a favor. You know that article you wrote last fall about the phone tracking scandal?"

"… Yes?" said the voice on the other end of the line.

"I need contact info for the bounty hunter you paid to track your phone."

Paul Sparrow was nominally a fellow reporter for *The Morning Watch*. 'Nominally,' because he'd written a series of articles over the past year that had brought him to the attention of several national news outlets. Most of his focus these days was on leveling up his career, but they were still technically coworkers. She liked him, and he had a painfully transparent crush on her, despite her best efforts to rein in the whole *supernatural influence* thing.

"*Um… okay?*" he said. "*Do I want to know why? Because I feel like I should warn you, that chick was super creepy.*"

"I'm not planning a slumber party with her," Neveah assured him. "I just need to find a missing person. And based on your article, she's pretty efficient at that kind of thing."

As part of his exposé on data insecurity in the cell phone industry, Paul had paid the bounty hunter in question three hundred dollars to acquire the location data for his phone—simply to show that it could be done by someone outside of law enforcement and in the absence of a warrant. The bounty hunter had taken less than an hour to come back with a map location a couple of hundred feet away from Paul's house.

Neveah had found it impressive at the time. Now, she hoped it could be directly useful as well.

"*Okay, if you're sure,*" Paul was saying. "*I can text you the contact info in a few minutes—I'll have to dig it out of the file. Just be careful, all right?*"

Neveah didn't tell him that the bounty hunter wasn't the one she needed to worry about—it was the person she was using the bounty hunter to try and find. Instead, she just said, "You're a star, Paul. Thanks—I owe you one."

They hung up after a brief exchange of *we should totally have lunch sometime* and *sure, maybe once I get to the bottom of this current story*. He was good to his word, and a text came through five minutes later with a first name, phone number, and email address.

Neveah texted the number immediately.

A friend of mine says you can trace phones. I have a private job, time sensitive, on a missing person. Cash up front, no law enforcement involved.

Two minutes later, the phone pinged.

Who's the friend?

Paul Sparrow, she typed back.

The reporter guy? came the reply. *This for another news story?*

No, Neveah texted. *Like I said, it's a private job. There's reason to believe the missing girl is at risk. Her parents are at their wits' end.*

The pause was much longer this time.

Okay, but the price has gone up. $1500, cash only.

Neveah didn't so much as blink. *Deal. I'm in Stockton. When and where can we meet?*

Another wait.

There's a tattoo parlor on Aurora, near Market St. Come at noon tomorrow and give the owner my name.

I'll be there, Neveah texted. She only hoped the delay wouldn't end up being a fatal one for any random humans that got in Alice's way.

━━━◆━━━

Neveah spent the night obsessively checking news articles and arrest reports from Calaveras County, while simultaneously fuming over the behavior of a certain demon. He was so *infuriating*, with his impenetrable emotional armor and his bloody-minded belief in his own moral infallibility.

Everyone is ultimately a means to an end, my ass, she thought mulishly. This, from someone who'd bound a fourteenth century Scottish nobleman as a servant because he'd thought it was funny, and then proceeded to keep the man around for company for the next six hundred years. What 'end' was Edward a 'means' to, in Nigellus' mind?

"Probably a means to ensure he always has someone to pontificate to, and doesn't end up talking to himself like a crazy person," she muttered, only to realize the irony a moment later. It made her even more irritated.

After accomplishing absolutely nothing of use overnight, she showered and changed first thing in the morning. To kill time while waiting for the meeting, she paid a visit to the back entrance of her favorite Japanese restaurant. The owner had thoughtfully left a couple of five-gallon jugs of used peanut oil for her car. After checking that the caps were tight, she stuck them in the hatchback, where the after-market heated filtration tank took up a sizable percentage of the hatchback. At least it meant she'd have enough fuel to chase down any leads in the general area without having to support the petroleum industry.

Once upon a time, she could have flown to her destination, her wings cutting through the dimensions to take her anywhere within moments. The memory of what she'd lost hurt, and she had to stop herself from trying to bring her wings out in the shadowed, empty alley, just to see if she could.

You're better off not knowing, she told herself firmly, and drew her focus back to the current mystery.

The rest of the morning dragged abominably. When noon finally rolled around, it found her at KT's Ink Emporium, a hole in the wall place inside a mid-century brick storefront with bars over all the windows.

A bell rang over the door as she entered, and a bored looking guy in his twenties glanced up from the magazine he was reading.

"Help you?" he asked.

"I need to speak to the owner, please," she said.

The guy craned around and called, "Yo, Katie! Someone in the front wants a word!"

A middle-aged woman with a square jaw and an aggressively gelled iron-gray mohawk stuck her head through the door leading to the back. "Yeah?"

"Hi," Neveah greeted. "I'm here to meet Celine. We have an appointment."

Katie jerked her chin in a beckoning motion. "She's expecting you. Come on back."

Neveah followed her, admiring the dragon tattoos that snaked down her arms, and trying not to think about the last full-sleeve tattoo she'd traced with her eyes and fingertips. The woman led her through the studio where she presumably did her work, and from there, to a second door leading into a small, cluttered office space.

Another woman awaited them inside, lounging against the wall next to a filing cabinet. Celine was also middle-aged, perhaps in her fifties—sleekly muscled, lightly tattooed, and with an evident fondness for leather and chains. Her shoulder-length auburn hair probably owed more to a dye bottle than to nature at this point, but her brown eyes were shrewd and piercing.

"Celine? I'm Neveah. Thank you for agreeing to meet me." Neveah reached out a hand and shook the bounty hunter's with a firm grip.

"Hey, fifteen hundred bucks is fifteen hundred bucks, right?" Celine said. "If you've got the money and the phone number you want traced, let's get down to it."

Katie gave them both a knowing glance. "I'll leave you to your client, babe. You know the drill—anything illegal, you take it someplace else."

Celine smirked. "Not illegal. Just questionably ethical, pet."

Katie left with a careless wave of one hand, closing the door behind her.

Neveah pulled out her phone and a wad of cash, passing the money over and waiting while Celine counted out the bills.

When the other woman gave a nod, Neveah texted her Alice's cell number. Celine's phone trilled, and she fished it out of her pocket to pull up the message.

"Got it. This is gonna take a little longer than it would have a year ago. You can thank your reporter friend for that. These days, the big telcos at least have to pretend that they're not selling customer data to anyone who asks. What used to be one giant database is now a bunch of smaller ones on the dark web, and there's some cross-referencing involved."

She typed something rapidly with her thumbs and sent it off.

"I've sent it on to my contact who takes care of this kind of shit for me. He'll get back with me once he has something, and I'll pass it on to you."

Neveah nodded. "Thank you. I'll keep an eye out for the message. In the meantime, I'm sure you have things to do."

Celine raised a pierced eyebrow. "Bit of a trusting soul, aren't you?"

With a shrug, Neveah replied, "Nah. Somehow, I doubt locking you in this room with me will make the process go any faster. And like you said, fifteen hundred dollars is fifteen hundred dollars."

Celine cracked a smile, huffing out a small breath of laughter. "That it is, sugar. I'll get back to you when I've got something. Hope you find your missing girl."

"I hope so, too," Neveah replied with the utmost sincerity. "She's had a rough time of it, and it's only likely to get worse."

She grasped Celine's hand in another brief handshake and headed out, thanking Katie on her way. Once outside, she paused, trying to decide on the best course of action while she was waiting. As much as it pained her, she was beginning to have second thoughts about the way she'd stormed off after the fight with Nigellus. She was still right and he was still wrong... but by burning that bridge, she'd ensured it would be much more difficult to keep tabs on what he was up to.

Neveah let herself into the Rabbit, settling back in the plush red velour of the seat. She tapped the steering wheel thoughtfully for a few moments, before deciding that it made sense to return to Vallecito while she was waiting for Celine to come through with the location info. No matter which direction Alice had headed when she ran off, that was where she would have started from. That meant it would also make the most efficient starting point for Neveah to chase after her.

And if she was going to Vallecito anyway, it wouldn't hurt to check up on her infuriating demon. Maybe she could still talk him around. And if not, she could at least get a feel for what progress he was making, if any. She turned the key in the ignition, letting the glow plugs heat up for a few seconds before cranking the engine. It sputtered into life, and she headed for the highway.

An hour and a half later, she still hadn't heard back from Celine. She turned onto the winery house's winding driveway. The property was still visible to her naked eye, and she took some comfort from the knowledge that Nigellus hadn't revoked her access to the wards. She parked in front of the shining glass-and-steel house, and walked up to the front door. Pushing the doorbell, she waited for Edward to appear and either let her in or tell her she was no longer welcome.

But nobody answered, and try as she might, she couldn't hear any sounds of life coming from within.

FIFTEEN

Edward tapped his fingers on the polished surface of the desk, his deeply lined brow furrowed in thought. "Alice's parents were no help, then?" he asked.

Nigellus shook his head. He'd spent half of the morning picking the couple's brains for anything useful, and come up blank. "No. They know next to nothing about their daughter's life since she went away to college. Between the police and their own disorganized efforts, all of the families of her childhood friends have been contacted, and none claim to have seen or heard from her. What about the credit card records?"

"There have been two cash withdrawals since the Seelie's body was found," Edward said. "The first occurred on the same day. The second was on the following day. Both took place at the closest ATM to Alice's apartment in Vallecito, and both were for the maximum allowable amount. There's been no other activity on the credit card since then."

So, Alice Ramirez had cash, and she'd been careful not to leave any clues as to where she was going. Nigellus dismissed that avenue of investigation as useless and cast around for the next. The options were quickly narrowing to one that would be deeply unpleasant on a personal level.

Edward sighed. "I could try to find out which officer is in charge of acquiring cell phone records. You could pry the information out of them and see if she's made any calls or texts that might help us find her."

"If she had, the police would have already have followed up on the leads," Nigellus pointed out. He growled in frustration. "These results are unacceptable. I need to speak to that blasted imp."

His human servant leaned an elbow on the desk. "You mean Leyak? That's going to be rather difficult without finding his heart first, isn't it, sir?"

"Difficult, yes," Nigellus replied. "Not impossible."

The stare Edward leveled at him wasn't amused. "You're about to do something rash. Do I even want to know?"

Nigellus waved it off. "Leyak needs a heart. I happen to have one. Under the circumstances, I will consider a loan."

Edward's expression screwed up in distaste. "On an exceedingly short-term basis, I hope."

"*Quite*," Nigellus said, the word bone-dry.

The scowl on Edward's face didn't abate. "I don't think much of this plan, but I don't suppose you were asking my opinion."

"Not really, no."

"Well, you're getting this much of my opinion, regardless," Edward said. "Wouldn't it make sense to track down Neveah and see if she's had any luck, before committing to something so radical?"

Something inside Nigellus balked at the idea of crawling back to the angel less than a day after she'd stormed off in a huff. His personal feelings on the matter were of little import in a situation so serious, but there were other considerations as well.

"It's a matter of timing," he said. "The angel is no more likely to have found Alice Ramirez in such a short period than we were. However, if she does somehow succeed, she will hide the human away in an attempt to protect her."

"Which will at least keep her out of Fae hands," Edward said slowly. "I see."

Nigellus gave a single, sharp nod. "I have a method for tracking her. However, it is only likely to work once more. I would prefer to use it *after* I've extracted the answers I need from Leyak."

"And after Neveah has more time to potentially find and secure Alice." Edward paused. "Two things. Firstly, I hope you weren't looking forward to any more romantic interludes with your angel, because when she figures out how you've tracked her, she's likely to hack off your manly bits and pack them away in salt."

"And secondly?" Nigellus prompted, in a tone that clearly said the first point wasn't a matter for discussion.

"The Fae controlling Alice's body has already put a bullet through Neveah's heart." Edward's tone was pointed. "Yes, she's immortal. But she's also severely weakened."

"That bullet wasn't intended for her," Nigellus said, refusing to let Edward's words plant a seed of doubt inside him. "She's also well aware of the danger the Fae poses. Weakened or not, she *is* one of the angelic host, while the Seelie is confined inside a human's body."

Edward's mouth turned down. "I don't like any of this. But when has that ever stopped you?"

"Rarely," Nigellus replied.

The human rose on creaking knees and paced across the room. "You're going to be terribly vulnerable while Leyak has your heart. I'm coming with you to Hell."

"Someone should stay here to monitor events," Nigellus said.

"Then send one of the lower demons up to do it," Edward shot back. "Melek, or someone else with experience on Earth. This isn't open for debate, sir."

It was unusual for Edward to put his foot down on a matter of import, even when they were in private. Nigellus pondered the logistics of bringing someone else to Earth to monitor police reports and news articles, then made his decision.

"If you insist," he said, and glanced at the clock. "It's almost noon. We should depart now; there's no benefit to putting it off."

"Very good, sir," Edward replied, once more the dutiful servant. "In that case, I'll just go and pack us a bag."

<hr>

Melek was once again on guard duty inside the gate when they arrived. "Back so soon, Nigellus? Is there news? Oh, hello, Edward."

"Hello, Melek," Edward replied.

Rather than answer Melek's question, Nigellus said, "I must speak to Baalazar again. Do you know where I might find him today?"

Melek drew himself up to attention, his tone growing formal. "I believe he'll be attending a meeting of the council in about twenty minutes, sir."

Nigellus nodded. "That is fortuitous. Please arrange for someone to replace you on watch and join us in the council chamber as soon as possible."

The guard blinked in surprise. "Me? Er… yes, sir. I'll be there shortly."

Edward and Nigellus exited the shallow cave system that housed Hell's side of the gate, emerging into the dry midday heat. Edward shaded his eyes with one hand and gazed down at the starkly beautiful valley below.

"Since we have a few minutes' grace, would you mind popping us into the titheling village for a brief visit, sir?" Edward asked. "I have a parcel for one of the residents there. It will only take a moment to pass it on."

Since there was no point in tracking Baalazar down early if he would just have to repeat everything to the rest of the council shortly afterward, Nigellus nodded his assent.

"Come, then," he said, and grasped Edward's arm. With a moment's concentration, he transported them to the dusty square in front of the building that served as the humans' communal meeting and governance hall.

The large double doors were open, and there seemed to be a fair amount of activity inside. The buzz of cheerful discussion emerged from the dim interior. Abruptly, Nigellus became aware of a subtle tug inside him. The connections in question were always there, in the same way as his connection with Edward was always present. However, it wasn't a bond he monitored at all times. These days, any attempt to do so would be unwelcome, to say the least.

Fatima, one of the village elders, emerged from the meeting hall. She stopped upon seeing him standing there with Edward.

"Nigellus," she said. "And Edward. Hello. Have you come to speak with the vampires?"

Edward perked up immediately. "Ransley and Miss Bright are here? Really?"

"For their scheduled blood donations, yes," Fatima said. She was a matronly human, middle-aged in appearance, with her olive skin and heavy brows proclaiming her Southeast Asian heritage.

This was a complication, though Nigellus couldn't deny the appeal of seeing the pair, even briefly. Unfortunately, that sentiment was unlikely to go both ways. At the end of the war, in the late eighteenth century on Earth, Nigellus had whisked Ransley away to safety in Hell as the Fae prepared to deploy their vampire-killing weapon. In the heat of the moment, Ransley had agreed to sell his soul to Nigellus in exchange for the survival of his vampire race — not realizing that under the circumstances, his survival *was* his race's survival.

When he'd learned that all of his fellows had been killed, Ransley had begged Nigellus to remove his memory of the both the war and the soul-bond he'd agreed to. Nigellus had pitied him enough to do so, and for more than two hundred years, he had maintained the ruse while quietly protecting the last vampire from harm.

Only recently had Nigellus' lie of omission come to light. Ransley had not taken it well, to put it mildly. To further complicate matters, Nigellus was now bound to Ransley's part-demon lover, Zorah Bright, as well. He had used that soul-bond to save both their lives when necessary, and he would continue to do so. In return, they agreed to provide Hell with the vampire blood the demons needed as a hedge against future conflict with the Fae.

As a part-bred succubus, Zorah could come and go from Hell as she pleased, and her bond with Ransley meant that neither of them required Nigellus' assistance for passage through the gate. These days, Nigellus only ever had contact with them when there was a crisis of some sort. As far as he was aware, Edward didn't have frequent dealings with them, either… but his elderly servant was already bustling inside with clear enthusiasm.

Nigellus followed—though he hung back, staying in the shadows by the door.

"Ransley! Zorah! What a wonderful surprise," Edward called, crossing the large hall.

Both vampires looked up sharply. Zorah released the wrist of a young woman she'd been drinking from, presumably to replenish herself after having her blood drained for Hell's coffers. "Edward?" She rose abruptly from her chair, swaying a bit before her legs steadied.

Ransley Thorpe rose as well. He was dark-haired and blue-eyed, his pale skin proclaiming both his English heritage and his vampire nature. By contrast, Zorah's complexion was dusky, and her shoulder-length hair curled in tight spirals. She hurried forward, meeting Edward halfway and throwing her arms around his frail shoulders.

"Hello, my dear," Edward replied, patting her back gently. "You're both looking well."

"You, too! Is Nigellus here with you?" Zorah asked.

Ransley sauntered up to them with a determinedly casual air, but his glacier-blue gaze was already locked on Nigellus. "Oh, he is indeed. Hello, Edward."

"It's good to see you, Ransley," Edward said, extracting himself from Zorah's embrace. "If somewhat coincidental. We're just here for a…" He stumbled a bit, his eyes sliding to Nigellus and away. "For a… meeting. I'd intended to drop off a package of coffee beans for young Sharalynn on our way to the council chamber."

Fatima, who'd been watching the exchange with Nigellus, stepped forward. "Coffee, you say? Give it here, you old reprobate, and I'll make sure she gets it."

Edward gave her a knowing smile. "Or at least most of it, eh?" Nevertheless, he rummaged in the bag he was carrying and handed over a paper-wrapped parcel. "Thank you, Fatima."

Since lurking inside the doorway was beginning to feel vaguely ridiculous, Nigellus joined the others despite being unsure of his welcome.

"Ransley. Ms. Bright," he greeted. "It is good to see you both. However, I fear we must take our leave in order to join a meeting of the Council, which is just about to begin."

Ransley closed the remaining distance between them, looking Nigellus up and down. "Interesting," he said, his British accent rich and precise. "Since I know for a fact that you despise council meetings almost as much as you despise being put on the back foot."

Nigellus regarded his one-time protégé without blinking.

Zorah joined them, leaning against Ransley's side with a forearm resting casually on his shoulder. "Hmm. It kind of makes you wonder if this meeting has something to do with the mysterious escaped prisoner that the villagers have been talking about."

Nigellus turned a sharp look on Fatima, who shrugged.

"If you want to keep news from spreading in Hell, I'm afraid you'll need to lock the place down a lot tighter than it is currently," she said, without any evidence of remorse.

"Few things travel faster than the speed of gossip in a small community," Zorah agreed.

"So true," Ransley agreed. "Mind you, the idea of 'escaping' from Hell is a rather interesting one, wouldn't you say? It implies there was a demon involved."

"It also implies that Hell keeps prisoners," Zorah put in. "You haven't exactly been advertising that little factoid, have you?"

Nigellus assessed this new wrinkle in the situation, calculating its risks and possible consequences. Edward shot him a look that clearly conveyed, *'at this point, you might as well tell them.'*

"Walk with us, please," he said, gesturing toward the large doors.

Ransley pinned him with a cool gaze for a long moment before relenting. "Very well."

Zorah straightened, pushing away from his shoulder. "We'll swing by again before we head out," she told Fatima. "Tell Sharalynn that I want to see her and Finn while we're here, okay?"

"I will," Fatima promised, giving them a measured smile before she excused herself, with Edward's package of Colombian dark roast cradled in her arms like a treasure.

Nigellus gestured again toward the door. The four of them went outside, heading for the edge of the small titheling village. The road beyond led toward the towering cliffs that held the council chambers and the demons' residences.

"Right, start talking," Ransley said. "Who is this prisoner, and why can't the demon who bound them teleport straight to them and recapture them?"

Nigellus took a breath and relayed a stripped-down version of the events of the past several days. He omitted the angel's involvement entirely, and left his own current plan for Leyak vague.

Though not, apparently, vague enough.

"Hang on," Zorah said. "If Leyak's heart is packed in salt and he's too weak to talk, how do you expect to get any answers out of him?"

Edward, who had been uncharacteristically silent on the walk, finally spoke up. "He intends to swap out the missing carburetor for an aftermarket model." He didn't sound pleased.

"Swap out the—" Ransley echoed. The vampire came to an abrupt halt. "You're going to tear out some other demon's heart so Leyak can use it?"

Zorah stopped, too. "Wait, *what*? Is that even a thing?"

"No," Nigellus said, with as much patience as he could muster. "I am not going to tear out some other demon's heart so Leyak can use it."

"He's going to let them cut out his," Edward said.

Zorah and Ransley stared at him. Nigellus turned and started walking again, cognizant of the passage of time. After a moment, the vampires hurried to catch up.

"You're genuinely worried that the war is about to start up again." Ransley's words were low and strained.

"I am, yes," Nigellus replied, since there was no point in lying about it.

"Well, *shit*," Zorah breathed.

Edward, huffing and puffing a bit at the pace, looked over at the pair. "I have a request for both of you, if you've nothing pressing requiring your attention on Earth."

"What is it, Edward?" Zorah asked softly.

"I'd like you to be present for this *procedure*, if you can call it that," he said. "Not to put too fine a point on it, but I'm concerned other demons might try to take advantage during a moment of extreme vulnerability, if you see where I'm going."

Ransley Thorpe had always had a rather disconcerting gaze, even when it wasn't lit from within by vampiric power. He turned those ice-blue eyes on Nigellus now.

"*Demon* and *vulnerability* aren't words you hear used in the same sentence very often," he observed, not breaking eye contact.

"Nevertheless," Edward said.

Nigellus wondered idly if Ransley was enjoying this, on some level. But apparently, that wasn't the direction his thoughts had taken.

"Handy to have the three people whose souls you have the power to reap nearby in case of emergencies," he said, mock-casual. "It's like bringing an emergency battery along, I suppose."

This time, it was Nigellus who stopped, rounding on his former protégé. "Oh, *please*. I am cognizant of the depth of your resentment and bitterness, Ransley, but that accusation is beneath you."

Rationally, Nigellus knew that anger was neither a useful nor an appropriate response to the verbal jab. Time was of the essence, and whether the two vampires decided to indulge Edward's paranoia or not, he needed to get to the council and lay out his case.

Zorah threaded her arm through Ransley's, looking up at him. "Be fair, lover. I think if he ever intended to use us as spare batteries, we'd already know about it." She met Nigellus' gaze and held it, a hint of copper fire flaring behind the brown of her eyes. "All right. We're in. Though—real talk, here—I'm not sure exactly what you expect us to do against a roomful of demons if things go south."

Edward smiled, though it didn't reach his eyes. "Not to worry, my dear. I think you two have more influence among the council than you really understand."

Above them, the carved sandstone cliffs loomed in the afternoon light.

SIXTEEN

The meeting place of Hell's Council of Six had been hewn by hand from the living rock over the passage of countless millennia. It was now a massive, echoing chamber, its domed ceiling rising a hundred feet or more above the stone floor. Intricate carvings decorated the walls—serpents and winged figures, great twining branches and geometric patterns all sharing space.

The mortal species from the other realms never truly appreciated the passage of time. There were a mere six hundred and sixty-six demons in existence, and aside from a rare handful of sterile human hybrids like Zorah, that was all there would ever be. Yet the demons had carved out this chamber and the hundreds of others like it, one painstaking chip of stone at a time.

Nigellus himself had contributed to the sculptures on the west wall, so long ago that the memories had grown hazy and soft-edged. These days, he was nominally one of Hell's rulers—the lowest demon within the first rank.

It pleased his people to organize themselves in groups of six, highest to lowest, for no other reason than that they chose to do so. Rank was not static, but neither was it prone to constant reshuffling. Nigellus, in his precarious perch at the bottom edge of the ruling Council, attracted more attention from ambitious lowers than most, and yet he had only fended off half a dozen challenges in the last thousand years.

The most recent challenger was currently languishing in dozens of dismembered pieces, scattered among a collection of abandoned salt mines arrayed across the human realm. Not dead—never dead, as a demon—but not currently a concern for Nigellus or those he considered under his protection.

Edward seemed convinced that another attempt on Nigellus' position might be imminent, given sufficient opportunity. Nigellus disagreed. This would be a private matter for the Council alone—or rather, for the Council and Leyak. And while not all of his fellow Council members were allies, the ones who weren't had nothing to gain from engineering Nigellus' downfall.

In short, he was useful to them, and therefore it was not to their benefit if he fell from his place.

The other Councilors had already arrived in the chamber, while Nigellus and his party were delayed in the human tithelings' village. Typhon and Mammon, his fellow demons of fate... Sabazius and Astaroth, both incubi... and of course, Baalazar, the sole imp residing within the first rank.

They were already seated at the long table that dominated the chamber, with Typhon in the place of prominence at the head. Nigellus swept in with his motley retinue at his back. He was the only demon in human form, as might be expected inside Hell. He could have transformed, of course, but doing so would have no bearing on what he'd come to do, and would probably disconcert the vampires.

Nigellus ruthlessly quashed an unwanted memory of the last time he'd worn his true form. Whatever the angel had done to his mind to engender lust, it seemed to be annoyingly persistent. It was also deeply inappropriate for the current situation.

"Greetings, Councilors," he said, the words resonating within the echoing chamber. "I wish to propose immediate action regarding the imp, Leyak."

"Nigellus." Typhon's voice was deep and booming. "You have further news, I take it?"

"I do," Nigellus replied.

"And why do you bring Earthens along to hear such sensitive information?" Typhon demanded.

"*Oy*," Zorah said, raising one hand. "Part-bred succubus over here, thanks very much."

"Not to mention, the source for keeping your vampire blood bank topped off," Ransley added. "I think we both have a vested interest in making sure the demons and the Fae don't start lobbing magical nukes at each other again."

"Edward requested the vampires' presence," Nigellus said. "He has... concerns regarding my proposed plan of action, shall we say."

Baalazar frowned. "What plan of action is this?"

"Allow me to relay the news first," Nigellus told him. "It is a theory only at this juncture, but the only one that fits all the facts. Upon escaping

Hell's gate, the Fae prisoner may have transferred her consciousness into the body of a human, commingling their spiritual essences as a way to escape her soul-bond with Leyak. Her physical form is most assuredly dead, but it appears that her mind lives on inside a human host."

Sabazius leaned forward. "So under this theory, it was the prisoner who set a trap for demons inside the human's apartment?"

"Indeed," Nigellus replied. "And if the human is able to reach a Fae and convince them of the truth—"

He let the sentence hang, watching as the implications sank in.

Mammon shifted his massive bulk, resting his elbows on the table. "You mentioned a plan of action."

Nigellus set aside his personal distaste for what he was about to propose. "Leyak can't answer questions with his heart missing. We have reason to believe that the prisoner has encased the stolen organ in salt to prevent him regenerating. I propose to give him my heart long enough for us to get the answers we need from him."

Typhon tipped his head to the side and regarded him with interest. Nigellus had surprised him, it seemed.

"You would *give* him your heart?" Baalazar echoed, as though to clarify.

"Perhaps 'loan' is a better word." Nigellus ignored the way Ransley's gaze was drilling a hole through the back of his neck. "I believe we should act immediately, as time is not on our side in this matter."

The imp shook his head slowly back and forth. "I knew you were worried, old friend. But *this*..."

Astaroth, ever the cool strategist, raised a hand to quell him. "No, it makes sense. And it saves the time involved in trying to find someone else willing to volunteer for something so..."

"Completely crazy?" Baalazar muttered.

"I was going to say unpleasant," Astaroth replied.

Footsteps echoed outside the chamber, and the guard Melek appeared in the doorway.

"Councilors," he greeted.

Nigellus spoke up before any of the others could question the guard's presence. "I've asked Melek here in hopes that he might travel to Earth and monitor the situation while I am indisposed. Edward, would you brief him on what he needs to know and ensure he has access to the housewards?"

"Of course, sir," Edward replied, and took Melek aside.

Typhon pinned him with a speculative look. "Well, Nigellus. If you are truly intent on this course, I suppose we should adjourn to Leyak's quarters." His glowing red eyes flicked to Ransley and Zorah. "Along with your vampire bodyguards, of course."

It was a casual barb, so Nigellus ignored it. Typhon was a warrior at heart. He always had been. He led the Council because no other demon was strong enough to best him, but Hell's defeat and the uneasy peace that had reigned in the centuries since the war galled him.

First and foremost, Typhon was a protector. He would not plunge Hell into a new war unless it was unavoidable. If the Fae made the first move, though—Typhon would lead the demons into battle with a view to settling old scores. Nigellus was determined to ensure things didn't come to that point simply because a single imp guard had exercised a catastrophic lack of judgment with a Fae prisoner.

Nigellus inclined his head in acknowledgement. "Lead the way. We can discuss the details of which questions need to be answered as we walk."

<hr>

Melek was promptly dispatched to the human realm with orders to report back immediately should Alice Ramirez surface within the human legal system. Nigellus would have preferred to have Edward doing the job, but the demon guard was competent enough with Earth technology and adept at following orders.

Leyak's living quarters within the sandstone cliffs were spacious and well kept, as was usual for a demon dwelling. Hell was not overflowing with natural resources, but until the Fae tithelings began to trickle in a couple of centuries ago, it had only needed to support six hundred and sixty-six inhabitants. With the Earth's plentiful resources right next door, no demon ever wanted for comfort and basic necessities.

Even so, the presence of the six Council members—along with a human and two vampires—crowded the space rather noticeably. Typhon ordered a second cot brought in and dismissed the incubus who'd been watching over Leyak's body.

Ransley approached the still form on the bed, looking down at him. The imp's skull was still grotesquely disfigured—only halfway knitted together. This, in addition to the gaping wound in his chest… the source of their current woes.

"Ugh," Ransley made a noise of distaste. "Poor bloke."

Nigellus examined the chest wound. Unbidden, an image of the angel clutching at the bullet wound in her chest as she lay on his marble floor flickered across his mind's eye. He wondered where she was right now, and whether she'd found any useful leads in his absence.

"This 'poor bloke' may yet end up precipitating a new war between the realms," Baalazar snapped.

Zorah scoffed. "In my experience over the past couple of years, the Fae are looking for *any* excuse to start things up again. If it wasn't this, it would have been something else."

Astaroth, who'd claimed a stretch of wall and was otherwise staying out of the way, shrugged. "They've been relatively quiet since the Wild Hunt went rogue. For a while, I was beginning to wonder if they'd lost their taste for saber-rattling altogether."

"It only takes a few bad apples to cause trouble," Ransley said. "Especially if they're in positions of power."

Two lower demons arrived, carrying a simple cot between them. The others pressed to the edges of the room, giving the pair space to set it down next to Leyak's bed.

Zorah eyed the cot with misgivings. "Can you really just hack out one demon's heart, stick in another demon's chest, and expect it to work? Because no offense, but that's pretty creepy."

"I fear it's not *quite* that simple," Nigellus said. "But as far as the end result goes, that is the general plan, yes."

Sabazius came forward to examine the imp's skull more closely. "It's going to take some time for him to utilize your heart's power and heal his brain enough to speak coherently. This won't be instantaneous."

Nigellus nodded. "Agreed."

There was a reason this sort of procedure was not common practice among demons. In Hell, everything was about power. Gaining it. Holding it. Using it. It went against demon psychology to give power away frivolously, especially when doing so strengthened another demon. Not only would Nigellus be making himself essentially helpless for the duration of the transfer; he would also have to resist the instinct to either pull his heart back from Leyak's body before their task of speaking with him was accomplished... or to pull power from other available sources.

These days, it was unusual for a demon to hold an active soul-bond with a native of Earth... much less with three of them. Before the treaty, soul-bonds were one of the principal ways for a denizen of Hell to gain power and status above his fellows. And in those long-ago times, the entire purpose of gathering soul-bonds was to use them.

Demons reaped. Perhaps not immediately or indiscriminately—but they *did* harvest what they'd cultivated. By contrast, Nigellus maintained his soul-bonds with Ransley Thorpe and Zorah Bright in order to protect them and ensure their lives continued. Nor would he ever consider giving up his servant Edward in exchange for a temporary power boost.

When Typhon cut out Nigellus' heart—for he would surely be the one to wield the blade—Nigellus' instincts would scream at him to pull sustenance from the souls he'd bargained for. However long the process of questioning Leyak took, he would be forced to fight that overwhelming impulse.

To say he wasn't looking forward to the experience was an understatement.

Typhon looked down at Nigellus' unprepossessing human form from his imposing seven-foot height. "You still wish to go through with this, spymaster?"

Nigellus swallowed a sigh and started unbuttoning his shirt. "Of course I do. As I said, time is not our friend in this matter."

Edward looked just about as unhappy as Nigellus had ever seen him, but he stepped close and took Nigellus' suit jacket and shirt for him.

"We'll be right here, sir," the elderly human said, stepping back.

Nigellus didn't reply as he crossed the short distance to the cot and eased onto it, rolling onto his back. As he'd expected, it was indeed Typhon who stepped forward, pulling a wicked ceremonial dagger from his belt.

"Whoa! Hang on just a minute," Zorah said, sounding alarmed. "You're going to do this *without anesthetic*? Nigellus, you can't be serious."

Baalazar answered, saving him the trouble. "Anesthetic? There's no drug in the three realms that could render a demon unconscious through something like this. It is what it is."

In his peripheral vision, Nigellus saw Ransley join Zorah, wrapping an arm around his vampire lover's shoulders and easing her away from the cot.

His blue gaze met Nigellus' and held. "As Edward said, we'll be right here, you slippery old bastard."

Nigellus was surprised by the depth of emotion he experienced in response to hearing his protégé's expression of solidarity—lukewarm and profanity-laced though it might have been.

"I've no doubt," he managed, and closed his eyes as Typhon raised the blade above his chest.

SEVENTEEN

Neveah debated trying to break into the winery house for an embarrassingly long time before finally talking herself out of it. On reflection, it seemed most likely that Nigellus and Edward were out following up with a lead on Alice, and the demon was far too canny to leave any clues behind for her to find if that was the case.

They were working at direct cross-purposes now, as much as the realization disappointed her. Neveah needed to find Alice before Nigellus did if she was to keep the human safe from a life sentence—or worse, a death sentence—in Hell. Meanwhile, Nigellus would be doing everything in his power to ensure that he found the human before she did, in order to fulfill his duty to the Demon Council.

After staring at the keypad for the advanced security system on the pristine white door for a long moment, she turned and walked back to her car. What she needed was a fresh break in the case. She pulled her phone out and checked it, despite the fact that she would have felt it vibrate if Celine had texted.

Nothing.

Neveah sat back in the driver's seat and quickly scrolled through news sites, looking for any new murders. Unfortunately, there were several—because this was California and that was simply the way humans were with each other. Without some other data point for cross-referencing, there was no way of knowing if any of the killings in several widely scattered cities were relevant to her search.

Her phone pinged. Neveah nearly dropped it in her haste to pull up the text notification.

"Finally," she grumbled, as Celine's number popped up.

Looks like your girl's phone is in Sacramento. Hopefully she's with it. Good hunting.

A map link followed. Neveah clicked it. The url opened to a mess of red location markers scattered across a wide area—but the largest cluster with the most recent timestamps was, as promised, in Sacramento.

Thank you, she texted back. *You're awesome and actually not creepy at all.*

A pause, and then the phone pinged again.

Don't spread it around, you'll ruin my rep.

Neveah replied with a zipped-lips emoji and locked the phone screen. There had been two murders in Sacramento in the last couple of days. With this new information in hand, that became suggestive. She started the car and headed for the highway, knowing she could be in Sacramento in ninety minutes or so if the traffic cooperated.

It was time to find Alice Ramirez before the Fae hiding inside her head caused any more loss of life.

Once Neveah found the right police station, she schmoozed her way inside to interview the lead homicide detective about the recent killings. Upon speaking with him, it didn't take long to discover that both murders had occurred in an area near a loosely connected group of tent communities. It was close to the end of the man's shift, and he was clearly keen to be rid of her. Even so, a judicious application of angelic charm yielded the fact that the two killings weren't considered a high priority.

"If we tripped all over ourselves trying to catch every homeless junkie who got high and killed their drug dealer, we'd never get anything else done," he said.

"Unhoused," she corrected automatically.

The man frowned. "Huh?"

"The preferred term for someone living in a temporary urban encampment is 'unhoused' or 'unsheltered,' not homeless," she told him in a distracted tone. Already, she was thinking about the best way to approach this situation, since it seemed likely Alice wasn't staying in a fixed location like a hotel or an acquaintance's residence.

"Whatever you say, lady," the detective told her. "Which newspaper are you with, again?"

"I'm a freelance journalist," she replied, not wanting to drag *The Morning Watch* into this mess. "Thank you for your assistance, detective."

"Sure thing." He paused. "So… um… can I get your number?" the man blurted. His face reddened, which might or might not have had something to do with the gold wedding band on his left ring finger. "In case I need to, y'know, follow up with you on any of this."

She stared at him until he squirmed, aware that it might be useful to have him as a contact despite her distaste at the idea.

"No," she said eventually. "But write yours down for me."

He grabbed a pen. "Great! Call me anytime. And I do mean *any* time."

She took the scribbled post-it note he handed her and left without another word, sparing a moment of sympathy for the guy's wife.

Her next stop was the city's largest newspaper—a well-respected publication that was faring better than most local news outlets these days. While it was tempting to charge straight into a feet-on-the-ground search for her target, she needed more information before going in cold.

"Hello," she greeted the smiling receptionist. "I need to speak with whoever covers the housing beat. I might have some information related to the recent murders around local tent encampments."

Of course, she had *plenty* of information related to the recent murders. Which wasn't to say she was planning on actually sharing any of it.

Fortunately, she was in luck—since the rhythms of a morning newspaper meant that many of the reporters were still in the office, readying their articles on the day's news for pre-press. The receptionist directed her to a desk near the back of the newsroom, where a harried-looking woman with dark hair escaping its bun looked up at her approach.

"Hello. Kathy Thornson?" Neveah asked. "Do you have a few moments to talk about the tent encampments in the city? I'm following up on two recent murders among the unsheltered community."

The reporter sobered. "Right. Messy business, that. Sure, we can talk—just give me five minutes to get my article filed first, okay?" She gestured to an empty chair nearby.

Neveah sat, waiting with as much patience as she could muster while the woman typed frantically at her keyboard.

A few minutes later, she hit the return key with an air of finality and looked up. "Deadline crisis averted," she said, with a faint smile. Her eyes caught on Neveah, taking her in properly for the first time, and Neveah let some of her aura slip out.

"I understand you cover the housing beat, and I need a quick primer on the area where these murders took place," she began. "Can you tell me about the people staying there?"

Kathy had already grown doe-eyed as Neveah's influence hit her. She opened her mouth and hesitated, as though she were having difficulty arranging her thoughts. "Um… well… it's basically a stretch along the El Dorado Freeway, Highway 50. Or under it, I guess I should say. There are access roads on either side of the freeway, with underpasses every block. Unhoused people set up tents and campers on the sidewalks beneath the highway deck, or park their cars there if they're living out of a vehicle."

"I see," Neveah told her. "Go on…"

The reporter licked her lips. "Well, it's a bit of a mixed bag when it comes to the folks staying there. Some are heavy drug users, but there are also families just trying to get by, and older people who got elbowed out of the job and housing market. The city used to sweep through and turf them out if there were any complaints from people living in the area, but there was a moratorium on evicting them after a big scandal last year. They're mostly left alone these days."

"The two recent murders were separated by several blocks, yes?" Neveah asked. "Any evidence they're connected?"

"Evidence?" Kathy echoed. "No. 'Evidence' would imply the police are investigating, which I'm pretty sure they're not." She shook her head in frustration. "As for whether they're connected, it's hard to say. The first death was close to a fairly decent residential neighborhood. But the second one was on the edge of gang territory. It could be a total coincidence that they happened barely more than twenty-four hours apart."

"That's unusual, though, isn't it?" Neveah pressed. "Two murders in two days?"

The reporter made a wavering so-so gesture with one hand. "Yes and no. Shootings in Sacramento sometimes come in spurts if they're gang related. Someone pisses off someone else, and all of the sudden it's full-out war. But like I said, the first murder wasn't close to gang territory."

Neveah nodded. "I see. Thank you, that's useful."

She rose.

Kathy frowned. "Be careful if you're going to dig into the one near 26th Street, okay? Someone *does* need to investigate stuff like this when the police can't be bothered to do it… but it's rough out there in certain parts of the city. They don't call it South Sac Iraq for nothing."

Being careful not to pack too much angelic power into it, Neveah offered her a smile. "Thanks for the warning, but you don't have to worry about me. I'll let you get back to your job, though I might be in again for another chat if I can't find the information I need."

The adoration lighting up Kathy's plain features didn't waver. "Okay," she said, a bit breathlessly.

Neveah left her, focusing once more on her phone as she headed out of the building and back to her car. She'd already marked the locations of the murders on her navigation app after talking to the police detective. Now, she searched for a map of gang activity in the city and compared them. As Kathy had said, one was near Blood territory, but not technically inside it.

The cell phone locator map Celine had sent her was a mess of little red markers, but when she zoomed in, the area they covered did, in fact, encompass both of the crime scenes. She would work on the hypothesis that Alice was hiding among the unhoused population, and, more tentatively, that she was living out of her car rather than a tent.

It was time to go talk to people in the area, armed with a photo of Alice that she'd pulled from social media. The residents in the encampments might not be in a hurry to speak with the police, but they'd talk to her. Everyone did eventually, once she let her true nature peek out to entice them.

<hr>

After some deliberation, Neveah decided to start at the scene of the first murder rather than the second. Alice was unlikely to be lurking around either location, and she had some vague idea that following in her footsteps might offer some kind of insight into her mindset... or rather, the Fae's mindset.

Unfortunately, one of the complications in dealing with possible witnesses who were living in makeshift shelter was that they could pick up and move rather easily. And, if the location she'd received from the detective was accurate, in this case, it looked like almost everyone had. The underpass at 18th and W Street was deserted except for a single, lonely tent made of tattered blue and silver tarps.

Evening shadows were beginning to darken the protected stretch of road beneath the freeway. She parked her car and approached the lone habitation on foot.

"Excuse me," she said to the skinny teenage boy sitting on a folding chair in front of the tent. "Can you tell me anything about the murder that took place here two nights ago?"

As she came closer, she saw the glass pipe hanging from the boy's hand, its bulbous end stained brown. His eyes were bloodshot and unfocused.

"Whoa," he said, after a longish pause. "Someone got killed here? Seriously?"

Neveah thanked him for his time and returned to her car. The next underpass yielded a larger number of people, including one family with small children. The tents here were proper camping gear, and they huddled close as though banding together against the growing dark.

After convincing the residents that she wasn't with the police and wouldn't be asking for anyone's names, she learned that the death had occurred after a man with a reputation as a troublemaker had attempted to steal from a woman none of them knew by name—newly arrived in the encampment with a nice car and enough cash to make her a tempting target.

"So it was self-defense?" Neveah asked.

The old man she was talking to shrugged his bony shoulders. "I mean, I expect she could have just shown him the knife instead of stabbing him in the gut and then slashing his throat. He wasn't armed. But he was going after her stuff, so... maybe?"

It seemed word of the second killing had reached this end of the encampment, as well. That victim's neck had been broken, which wasn't exactly the hallmark of a standard gang killing. Neveah was now quite confident that Alice's Fae hitchhiker was behind both deaths. The question would be whether or not she'd stuck around the area afterward. Leaving Sacramento would have been the obvious thing to do, but the cell phone time stamps showed she was still in the area as of mid-morning today.

The last time the Seelie had been on Earth, human laws and the attitudes toward murder in the American West had been a much different thing than they were today. Alice would know better, of course, but there was no telling whether or not the Fae was drawing on her host's knowledge—not beyond the nuts and bolts of driving cars, acquiring cash, and utilizing modern firearms to construct *really irritating* booby traps, anyway.

What Neveah really wanted to know was the Seelie's endgame. She was wandering around in a world that must be nearly unrecognizable to her. Neveah figured she would be looking for other Fae, but Alice would have no useful knowledge to help her with that. The Seelie wouldn't have any way of knowing that most major cities now had Fae operatives working behind the scenes to maintain their shadow control of Earth and humanity.

She wondered if the Seelie was trying to make for Seattle, where the Fae had maintained a presence among the native Duwamish tribes toward the end of the war. If so, that might give Neveah a bit of leeway when it came to tracking her down before she could reach others of her kind.

Of course, this assumed the trail of murders didn't draw the wrong kind of attention. The Fae presence in Northern California was lighter than in many other places on Earth these days, simply because of its proximity to Hell's gate. But even so, there was a Fae overkeep based in San Jose, and another one in Los Angeles. Had the escaped Seelie only known that, she could already have contacted her people by now.

Neveah thanked the man she'd been speaking with. Next, she went to check the location of the second killing near 26th and X Street. The area was completely devoid of tents and campers, but not of people. Hard eyed young men—wearing red clothing and conspicuously failing to conceal the guns they carried in their waistbands—watched her drive past with stony expressions.

Gang territory.

Not technically, perhaps—but it looked like whatever had happened last night was sufficient to have them out patrolling beyond their usual haunts. Neveah drove a couple of blocks west until she found more tents. The denizens here were on edge. Some of them were packing up despite the late hour, taking down tents by the light of battery-powered lamps.

A careworn middle-aged woman gave her a long look. "You wanna get out of here, girl. There's trouble brewing tonight."

"Oh? Can you tell me what's going on?" Neveah asked, keeping her body language open and unthreatening.

"The Oak Park Bloods are out here lookin' for someone," said the woman. "And whoever it is, I wouldn't wanna be them."

"Oh, dear," Neveah said. "That's not good." She drew breath to ask who they were after, but the words were cut off by a flash of unearthly light from somewhere beyond the underpass, followed by a rolling wave of power that tingled along Neveah's nerves like champagne bubbles.

The woman whirled. "What the *shit*—?" she began... but Neveah was already running.

She emerged from the underpass, taking in her surroundings. The flash had come from the direction of a construction area on the south side of the freeway, fenced off with temporary chain link panels on rickety-looking posts. The area was half-hidden under a spaghetti bundle of exit ramps, with another major highway running at right angles a few hundred yards beyond. An empty parking lot on the far side of the outer road offered the only clear vantage point where humans might have seen what happened in any detail. It appeared deserted—she couldn't see or sense anyone nearby.

Neveah slowed, trying to feel out the residual magic in the air and follow it to its source. She couldn't afford to focus on the implications of magic having been used in the first place. Not until she tracked down the epicenter of the blast.

Angel eyes could have managed well enough in the dark, but anemic streetlights illuminated a large section of the fenced-off site. The chain link on one of the panels was loose at the bottom, the regular diamond pattern of its mesh squashed and irregular where it had peeled back from the post, forming a gap. Neveah squeezed through the tight space without even pausing, tasting the tang of inhuman power against her tongue.

On a stretch of dirt where the concrete had been torn up between half a dozen massive cylindrical highway support beams, several figures lay sprawled on the ground. Five young men in red clothing were arrayed in a rough half-circle surrounding a single dark-haired woman.

None of them were moving.

EIGHTEEN

Nigellus lay on the cot in disconnected agony, unmoving and unseeing. In the bed next to him, his heart beat in Leyak's chest, lending the imp strength to heal the rest of his wounds over the course of hours instead of weeks.

He could feel every rhythmic pulse of the muscle, and his instincts cried out to wrench it back through the ether, into his wide-open ribcage where it belonged. The soul-bonds leading to Edward, Ransley, and Zorah twanged with tension—potential energy waiting for his use. He clamped down on the temptation, locking it away from his awareness as much as he could under the circumstances.

Ransley sometimes liked to quote the human Bible, telling people that Nigellus was legion; that he contained multitudes. It was both the truth, and also deeply misleading. In some ways, the countless humans whose souls he'd reaped across the millennia lived on via the medium of his own immortality. But in other, more meaningful ways, they were gone, their animus—their life force—expended in the pursuit of whatever purpose Nigellus had needed it for at the time.

They did not whisper to him like ghosts, offering counsel from beyond the grave. He retained nothing but his own memories of them, to whatever degree they had made an impression as their souls sunk into him to fuel his well of power.

Those days were gone. The bonds he held now were not for that purpose. Not even when his bloody heart had been ripped out through shattered ribs and given to another.

This would only be for a short time. His heart would be returned when Leyak answered their questions, and as a demon of fate, Nigellus had other sources of power besides Edward and the vampires. The energy inherent in this wrinkle in fate's turning had been sinking through his skin ever since Baalazar first appeared in his house in Atlantic City to relay the news of the Seelie prisoner's escape.

He lacked the vigor to open his eyes. In fact, he couldn't move at all. His muscles held no strength, but he could still hear—even if the sounds reached him as though coming through a long and twisting tunnel.

A hand clasped one of his, fingers intertwined. He could feel the pressure against his skin, if not the texture. That had been unexpected, if only because the grip was too strong to be Edward's. Besides, Edward would know better. Nigellus would chide him endlessly for that kind of sentimentality, especially in front of the Council.

No... the hand holding his belonged to Zorah Bright, of all people. He had no idea what she could possibly have been thinking. Idly, he wondered what Ransley's opinion of the gesture might be.

Abruptly, the atmosphere in the room changed. A chair scraped against the stone floor. Zorah's hand tightened on his with vampiric strength.

"He's waking up." The words were twisted and attenuated as they reached his ears, but he vaguely recognized Baalazar's voice.

Nigellus' disconnected heart labored as Leyak stirred; he could track the imp's progress toward consciousness by how hard it was pounding.

"*Leyak.*" Typhon's booming voice demanded attention.

Leyak's strangled groan was the same sound that would have come from Nigellus' throat, if he could only draw breath to make it.

"Wh-what happened?" the imp rasped.

"You tell us." That was Baalazar again. "You were tasked with guarding an important prisoner. Explain to us exactly what you did."

A sharp, indrawn breath. "*Oh.* Oh, no…"

"Talk, imp." Typhon, again. "The Council demands a full report, and you are currently on borrowed time."

"Oh, fates. What have I done?" Leyak's voice wavered. Nigellus wanted, rather badly, to shake him and tell him to get to the bloody point.

"You entered into a soul-bond with the unnamed Seelie," Baalazar said impatiently. "Tell us why you would do such a thing, and then tell us what happened next."

"She said a soul-bond would help her regain her memory so she could explain herself to the Council." The imp sounded utterly miserable. "She wanted to return to Dhuinne. She said maybe you'd be lenient and allow her to leave Hell if she was able to cooperate."

"And you agreed to do this without consulting anyone, *because*…?" Baalazar's tone sounded deeply unamused.

"She said it would also enhance my status if I could help her give you the information you wanted. B-but then, she touched my forehead and suddenly I couldn't seem to think straight."

"Did she say anything after that?" Typhon demanded.

A hesitation. Then, "She said she'd renounced her name and her memories so she could come here in secret to learn the demons' weaknesses. She said the Fae Court might have been willing to bargain and appease after the war was over—but that she wouldn't be content until she'd destroyed Hell utterly."

Silence fell heavily, broken only by the low, buzzing whine in Nigellus' ears. Misgivings tugged at him, urging him with renewed urgency to swill power through his bonds and heal himself.

"Did she say who she was?" Baalazar asked, so quietly Nigellus could barely make out the words. "Leyak, *did she give a name?*"

Another maddening pause, before Leyak said, "I'm so sorry. I'm *so sorry*—I didn't mean for any of this to happen!"

"Answer the question, Leyak!" Typhon bellowed. "*Who was this Seelie?*"

Nigellus' missing heart thudded and skipped beneath the force of Leyak's mortification.

"She called herself Dhuinne's Midwife," the imp said despondently.

"*What*?" Ransley hissed, in the instant before all the Council members started talking at once.

Nigellus' entire body twitched as the utter impossibility of the revelation warred with an avalanche of potential repercussions. He wrenched his heart out of Leyak's chest and pulled its component atoms through the ether, drawing it back into himself before he'd fully registered his decision to do so. His willpower hung by a thread as he held back the soul-bonds, not touching them for fear that allowing a single drop of power to leak through would shred his control completely.

Leyak cried out and started thrashing as his borrowed heart slipped away. Nigellus ignored him, pulling back that which was his and nobody else's.

"Who the hell is Dhuinne's Midwife?" Zorah asked, sounding bewildered.

It was Ransley who answered, since the others were still talking over each other; a frantic background babble. "The Midwife of Dhuinne is a sobriquet; one you'd recognize if you knew your Shakespeare. It's a *nom de guerre* of the Fae Queen, Mab."

"Holy shit, are you *kidding* me?" Zorah demanded. "Queen Mab, as in the same bitch who ordered the Vampire Killer to be used during the war?"

"That's the one," Rans replied in a tightly controlled tone.

Nigellus' heart reformed in his chest, the flesh knitting together far too slowly. His entire consciousness narrowed to a single point as the most appalling implication of all set in.

Edward leaned over him, clutching his shoulder. "Sir. We left Neveah chasing after her. She doesn't understand who she's dealing with."

Nigellus clenched his jaw, struggling to heal himself without drawing from the vampires or his servant... still unable to speak. His impossible angel—so weakened by time and separation from her native realm that a single salt-packed bullet had nearly discorporated her. And Nigellus had left her on Earth, in order to come here and weaken himself beyond usefulness.

Neveah was alone with the most powerful Fae that Dhuinne ever produced, and she had no idea.

"Neveah?" Zorah echoed. "As in, Neveah Lane? The weird chick who was stalking you a couple of years ago? What does she have to do with this?"

"Long story," Edward said, strain audible in his voice. "But right now, he needs to get back to Earth. *Fast.*"

Nigellus managed to blink his eyes into focus, still unable to speak or rise.

"Er, no offense," Zorah said, "but he doesn't look like he's going to be going anywhere at the moment—fast or otherwise."

"Neveah Lane is attempting to track down Alice Ramirez?" Ransley asked.

"Yes," Edward replied tersely. "And the Seelie hiding inside Alice has already made one spirited attempt to kill her."

"Then why on Earth did you let her go alone?" Zorah demanded. "Good god—I've met the woman, and she looks like a stiff breeze could blow her over. She's, like, barely a hundred pounds sopping wet!"

"As I said, it's a long story," Edward said. "Sir, you need to pull yourself together faster than this. If you have to draw animus from me—"

"No." Ransley's flat declaration cut him off. "Move aside, Edward—give me some space."

"What are you doing?" Zorah asked.

"Giving him vampire blood," Ransley replied. "And yes, I'm aware of the irony."

Baalazar moved into Nigellus' limited field of vision. "You do realize I wasn't done questioning Leyak when you yanked your heart back, Nigellus?" he asked peevishly.

Ransley's voice was grim. "I doubt anything else you might have pried out of him would have topped the 'Queen Mab' revelation."

The dark-haired vampire loomed over Nigellus' cot. His ice-blue eyes glowed, lit from within by vampiric power. Baring razor-sharp fangs, he used them to tear into his own wrist. A thin stream of blood dripped into Nigellus' open chest cavity.

"Here," Zorah said, leaning over him from the other side. "I'm one-quarter demon. My blood might work better." She repeated Ransley's actions, her brown eyes glowing molten copper as she unleashed her power. More blood trickled over his shattered ribs and exposed heart.

Vampire blood was a concentrated source of healing, able to repair humans' wounds and even extend their life spans. There was a reason it was one of the most sought-after substances in existence, as well as being one of the rarest.

Nigellus—already an immortal—couldn't utilize it in the same way a human might. But blood also carried raw animus, the medium of life. By bleeding for him, Ransley and Zorah were giving him some of their life force, offering freely what he did not dare take without consent through the soul-bond.

He grasped the power greedily, safe in the knowledge that he couldn't accidentally lose control and take too much. His body drank in the animus, directing its energy to knit flesh and bone and sinew together, reassembling his human guise.

It wasn't enough to complete the job perfectly, but it would suffice for now.

He rolled into a sitting position, one hand clutching at the ugly scar on his chest. Edward shouldered past Ransley to steady him.

"Sir—"

Except for Baalazar, the others were still arguing over the proper response to Leyak's disastrous revelation. If fate was with him, he'd be able to get to the angel before she found Alice. It had barely been more than a day, after all.

"We're leaving," Nigellus said. With no further warning than that, he teleported to the gate, pulling Edward along with him.

His servant didn't comment on the abrupt departure, following him past the guards on duty without argument, and onward through the passage leading to Earth. The human pulled out a small flashlight and flipped it on, playing it around the familiar underground passage.

"Just go to her, sir," Edward said. "You're still badly weakened, and I can make my own way back to the winery house. Find her before she finds Alice, and I'll meet both of you there."

Nigellus nodded, not wasting energy on speech. He focused inward, looking for the tiny thread that still remained to link him to the small amount of his essence that he'd left inside the angel.

A lie of emission, he thought grimly, and dragged his aching body through the ether, following that single, silken thread.

NINETEEN

Neveah stared at the motionless figures on the ground, frozen for several precious seconds as the implications of what she'd just experienced settled in. The Seelie had used magic, despite being trapped in a human body.

How was that even possible?

Alice lay in a crumpled heap, her dark hair covering her face. Around her, the five gang members' bodies sprawled as though they'd been physically blown backwards. Three of them still had guns held loosely in their hands. The neck of one was obviously broken.

Neveah moved from one fallen figure to the next, checking pulses. All were dead. She didn't see any obvious marks on the bodies, but the tang of ozone and magic hung heavy in the air. Finally, she crouched next to Alice, entirely unsure what to expect. The girl's pulse beat strong and steady beneath Neveah's fingers. Her eyes darted restlessly beneath closed lids.

There were two possibilities. Either the Fae was still in control of Alice's body, or her current state of unconsciousness meant that this was Neveah's chance to reach the human's awareness after the Seelie weakened herself by casting such powerful magic.

It was a gamble, but one Neveah was willing to take. She patted Alice down for weapons, relieving her of a viciously sharp steak knife that had very likely been used to slit two people's throats. Next, she found a loaded semiautomatic pistol—possibly lifted off the gangbanger she'd killed the previous night.

After wiping down both handles to remove any incriminating fingerprints, she tossed them behind one of the massive concrete support columns nearby. After a moment's consideration, she dumped the gang members' weapons there as well. Neveah was banking on the fact that even if the Seelie was still in control, she wouldn't be able to summon any magic strong enough to be dangerous to an angel. Not so soon after knocking herself out with the last attack.

"Alice," she said, returning to the human's side. "Wake up."

She gave Alice's shoulder a gentle shake. At first, there was no response, but then Alice groaned. Neveah helped her roll onto her back, smoothing tangled hair away from her face. A smear of dust marred her cheek, which showed the beginnings of a spectacular bruise from her fall.

Alice grunted softly and winced, lifting a hand to her head. Brown eyes blinked open, struggling to focus.

"Wh-where am I?" she croaked. "What happened?"

Neveah sat back on her heels. "You're in Sacramento, and as for the rest, it's probably best if you don't ask quite yet. Are you hurt? Do you think you can stand up if I help you?"

"I… don't know." A quaver of uncertainty lay beneath the words. "Who are you?"

"Call me Nev," Neveah told her. "I'm here to help. Come on, give me your hand."

Neveah used the grip to haul Alice into a sitting position. From there, she rose, pulling the human up with her. "There you go. Well done."

Alice swayed, but after a moment she locked her knees and gave a tentative nod. "Okay. I think I'm okay. Thanks."

Neveah had deliberately kept her facing away from the half-circle of dead men lying on the ground around them. Unfortunately, the gang members had pinned Alice against the fence right before she went off like a Fae-powered bomb. To get out, they were going to have to turn around and walk past the bodies.

"Erm… I don't suppose I could get you to close your eyes for this next part?" she asked.

Alice frowned. "What? Why?"

She spun around to look, nearly losing her balance in the process. Neveah steadied her, which was just as well since she staggered backward in the next instant, her shoulders hitting the fence with a rattle of chain link.

"Oh my god," Alice squeaked. "Oh my *god*!"

Neveah took her by the arms, standing in front of her to block her view. "Alice. They tried to attack you. We can't help them now, but we need to get you away from here, to someplace safe. Is your car nearby?"

"M-my car?" Alice swallowed hard. "I can't remember. My brain feels all weird, like—" She cut herself off, lifting a hand to her head again.

"You drove to Sacramento from Vallecito," Neveah told her, taking advantage of Alice's distraction to wrap an arm around her shoulders and lead her through a gap between two of the bodies. "You stayed in a tent community set up beneath the freeway."

"Oh," Alice said blankly, stumbling along in the direction Neveah led her. "My car. There's something…" She trailed off for a few seconds before breathing in sharply. "My *car*. I wanted to leave last night, but the transmission is busted. It slips out of gear if you try to go more than twenty-five miles per hour."

Another part of the puzzle slotted into place. Alice had made it as far as Sacramento on her way to wherever the Seelie was trying to go, but now she was stuck. She could drive a few blocks on the side streets, moving from one underpass to another. But she couldn't get on the highway and leave. She almost certainly didn't know how to steal a car, and while she might have cash, it probably wasn't anywhere near enough for transmission repairs.

"Were you heading north?" Neveah asked, knowing as a journalist that it was dangerous to ask leading questions—but desperate for Alice to remember more.

"I… think so?"

They'd reached the damaged section of fence. Neveah left Alice to stand on her own for a moment as she wrenched at the crumpled chain link, widening the gap.

"Okay," she said. "Here's what we're going to do. My car is a little over a block from here—not far. We're going to a motel for the night, and then I have a friend who I think can help you." She would have to contact the cat-sidhe again as soon as they got to safety. With luck, the little Fae could meet them at a different location this time, since Nigellus already knew about the Devil's Pulpit.

She squeezed through the newly widened gap, and Alice followed.

"My parents," Alice said.

Neveah winced. Notifying Alice's parents would basically be the same as notifying the police.

"Let's see about getting them a message in the morning," she hedged. "Speaking of which, can I see your cell phone for a second?"

Alice handed it to her, still looking dazed. Neveah tried to power it on and confirmed it was completely dead. It was possible that the battery was drained, but more likely that the blast of Fae magic had fried the circuitry.

"Looks like it's out of commission," she said, handing it back.

Alice frowned at it. "Must've broken it when I fell, I guess." She wavered on her feet again, catching herself on the nearest fence post. "Uh... I really don't feel well..."

Neveah had just opened her mouth to say something reassuring when she felt the air pressure change behind her. She whirled to find Nigellus standing a few feet away, only to blink in surprise as she took in his appearance. The demon was bare from the waist up, and a fresh, jagged scar bisected his chest. His skin was pale with the same sort of near-translucence that she'd seen in the mirror after the Seelie's bullet had pierced her through the heart.

Alice shrieked at the sudden appearance of a half-naked man out of thin air.

Neveah grabbed her by the arm, pushing her back a step. "It's all right. Stay behind me."

"Neveah." Nigellus' voice was a hoarse rasp. "Step away from her."

She tightened her grip, assessing their surroundings for possible escape routes. "Yeah, sorry, that's not happening. How did you even track me here? And what on *earth* happened to you?"

"Nothing on Earth," Nigellus said. "Move away. The Seelie possessing Alice Ramirez is *Mab*, Neveah."

Neveah stared at him with her mouth open for a beat. "*What?*" Her voice rose to a shrill shout despite her best efforts to moderate it. "You were holding the fucking *Queen* of the *Fae* prisoner in Hell?"

Alice cringed back in Neveah's grip.

"What are you talking about?" she said, her tone high-pitched and terrified. "What's *happening*? Who is this guy? He just appeared out of no-where!"

Nigellus didn't even spare her a glance. "She's dangerous, and not just to the humans. She is dangerous to every inhabitant in the three realms, and I need to take her back to Hell *now*. So *step away*."

It was exactly what Neveah had feared all along. Alice cowered behind her—confused, terrified, and oh-so-very human. The demons would sacrifice her without thought in an attempt to safeguard their secret… a secret far more terrible than any of them had guessed. Mab had already escaped Hell once. Only a fool would believe the Council would leave her alive to make a second attempt.

"No," she told Nigellus, not backing down or letting go of Alice. "Look at her. She's human, and she's an innocent. I will not let you sacrifice her as part of a political cover-up!"

"You won't stop me," Nigellus warned. "Move aside, Neveah… or I *will* move you myself."

TWENTY

Neveah weighed her strategic options, aware that none of them were terribly good. "Alice," she said, very deliberately, "I'm going to protect you. But you must not, at any cost, let this man touch you. Stay back, and don't let him get within arm's reach."

If Nigellus got a hand on her, he'd be able to teleport Alice away before Neveah could stop him. Meanwhile, the poor human was choking on terrified tears, her arm shaking violently in Neveah's grip.

"I don't understand what's happening!" she said. *"Why can't I remember what happened to me?"*

Nigellus' cool amber gaze slid past Neveah to land on Alice. "You are suffering from a very specific mental condition, Ms. Ramirez. You are not at fault, but until you receive treatment, you're placing other people in danger. I can help you, but for that, you must come with me."

The demon's tone was reasonable, but Neveah recognized the compelling resonance behind it. Alice leaned forward, straining unconsciously closer to that siren song of mental influence.

"Oh no you don't," Neveah snarled, incensed that Nigellus would even consider using mind control on a girl whose brain had already been

victimized so terribly. She dug her fingers into the human's arm. "Alice, snap out of it!"

Alice gasped and reeled back. Neveah catalogued the response with a degree of unease, because a normal human would *not* have been able to break the compulsion so easily. This entire thing was going to be a balancing act, made more dangerous by the revelation of exactly which Fae had hijacked Alice's mind and body. But Neveah was damned if she'd let Mab's victimization be compounded further by the Demon Council's desperation to hide what they'd done.

Nigellus' piercing eyes pinned her. "This is what you will be loosing on the people of Earth if you persist in this course, angel. Are you truly willing to risk it? You will not be able to control her once Mab takes over her mind again."

He was still talking, and that fact prickled at Neveah's instincts. Why bargain with her rather than teleporting across the short distance separating them and grabbing Alice before she had time to react?

"You've been weakened," she realized. "Badly. I don't know what you did, but you don't have enough energy for your usual demon tricks. You didn't expect to find Alice here with me, did you?"

"Perhaps not," Nigellus said. "But her presence is fortuitous nonetheless."

It hadn't even been thirty-six hours since Neveah stormed off after the meeting with the catsidhe. At the time, neither she nor Nigellus had possessed any useful leads regarding Alice's location. He'd come here immediately after whatever had caused that horrible scar on his chest, probably intending to warn her about Mab and convince her to abandon the chase.

Neveah narrowed her eyes at him as another connection slid into place. "You came straight here, which means you're still holding onto a physical connection between us. You *lied to me*, Nigellus."

"I did what was required to perform my duty to the Council," he replied stiffly, making her think she'd hit a nerve.

Alice jerked weakly against Neveah's hold on her arm. "Please let me go," the girl rasped. "Both of you. Let me go... I haven't done anything!"

Neveah chanced a quick glance at the human. Tears were streaming down her cheeks.

"No?" Nigellus asked. "Tell me, Ms. Ramirez—how is your landlady's health these days?"

Alice went still as a statue. A faint gasp, barely audible, indicated that the question had hit home. "I... I don't..."

Righteous rage flooded Neveah's chest in response to the unnecessary cruelty. At the same moment, a crazy idea entered her head. It would be madness to attempt it in the normal course of things, but right now, Nigellus looked like a ghost.

How weak was he?

She was about to find out.

"That's it," she snapped. "No more manipulation. You and I are done here, demon."

She released Alice, who immediately tried to run away, stumbling over her own feet in her haste. Nigellus tensed as though to give chase despite his weakness—either physically or by teleporting—but

Neveah lunged forward and slapped a palm against the ugly, half-healed scar over his heart.

Calling on abilities she hadn't used in centuries, she reached into the warren of pocket dimensions beyond the physical, following the path through the demon's awareness and searching for a very specific item.

Once, the thing she sought had been as much a part of her as her wings. She summoned that lost part of herself with all of her waning angelic power, demanding that it return to her. With one hand still pressed to Nigellus' skin, she reached out with the other, fingers open and ready.

The sword hilt materialized in her grip, solid and a lot heavier than she remembered it being. She readjusted her stance, giving Nigellus a hard shove backward as the three-foot long flaming blade burst into physical reality.

Alice screamed in terror and fell to the ground perhaps thirty feet away, curling into a fetal position with her hands over her head. Nigellus stumbled back a step, gaping at his stolen weapon.

"That's impossible," he breathed.

Neveah twisted her wrist, swinging the fiery blade in an easy figure eight motion—trying not to let on how much of a strain it was to wield the heavy sword, when she had once found it effortless. She moved deliberately between Nigellus and the human cowering on the ground.

"Why would it be impossible?" she taunted. "This is Shemasiel's blade, isn't it?"

Nigellus watched her warily.

"Well," she continued. "I'm Shemasiel. Or at least, I was in another life. So, anyway, thanks for giving me my sword back."

The demon continued to stare for a long, pregnant beat.

"You do surprise me, angel," he said eventually.

Neveah pasted on a fake smile. "I try," she said. "And I apologize for this next bit, because you already look like mortality warmed over. But I need a head start, and I doubt you'll give me one just because I ask nicely."

Nigellus didn't move. His heavy gaze held hers unblinkingly. "She will destroy you, Neveah. And then she will destroy everything else. You don't fully appreciate who—or what—you're dealing with."

Neveah shook her head. "No. You don't get to play that card, demon. This isn't about a mad queen; it's about an innocent human. You could have helped me find a way to fix this injustice. But since you won't, I'll do it myself."

With that, she let the fiery blade fly. Nigellus dodged, giving ground, but did not teleport away from her—proof positive that he was running on fumes. Neveah lunged, compensating for her own relative weakness and relying on millennia of experience to guide the blade. Nigellus skipped backward again, but too slowly. The sword hissed through the air and buried itself in flesh, just above his left knee. Neveah grabbed the hilt two-handed and heaved, cleaving through bone.

The demon cried out and fell to the ground, his leg nearly severed through.

Panting with exertion, Neveah banished the sword to a new dimensional hiding place—one that would be well out of his reach, with luck. The contact with a familiar artifact from her native realm had sent a burst of unaccustomed power thrumming through her veins, though it would probably be short-lived. She glared down at her vanquished foe, teeth bared. Nigellus looked up at her, wordless, his jaw clenched tight in pain.

"You can take back the rest of your tracking jizz, as well," she bit out, using the unexpected boost of power to reach inside herself and isolate the tiny part of his essence still remaining within her body. "And can I just say—that really was *incredibly* rude."

She expelled it with extreme prejudice, the demonic material burning away to nothing beneath the force of her irritation.

He flinched.

"Goodbye, Nigellus," she said coldly. "Look me up sometime, if you ever decide to stop treating sentient beings like disposable chess pieces."

With that, she turned and jogged toward Alice's huddled form.

"Up," she ordered, needing to be well away from the injured demon by the time he pulled himself together enough to pursue them. Alice whimpered as Neveah dragged her to her feet and slung the human's arm across her shoulders. "We're going somewhere safe, and then I'm contacting someone who can help you."

She projected as much angelic reassurance as she could muster, aware that Alice had already shrugged off a not-inconsiderable dose of demonic mental control tonight. Either it worked, or Alice had shut down completely and was operating in pure survival mode. Whatever the case, she let Neveah guide her west along the outer road, toward the underpass where she'd left the Rabbit parked.

When they reached the elderly Volkswagen without any immediate sign of demonic pursuit, Neveah swallowed a sigh of relief. She eased Alice into the passenger seat, buckling her in before hurrying around and jumping into the driver's seat. The engine stuttered and coughed before catching, but then the sound settled into its familiar rumble.

"Where's your car?" she demanded, once they were a couple of blocks farther away from the incapacitated demon.

"21st Street," Alice whispered.

Neveah watched the street signs and turned right at the underpass, driving past a couple of ancient campers. "That one?" she asked, as they approached an unremarkable midsized sedan. Alice nodded dumbly.

She pulled over, but left the engine running. "Keys," she said tersely.

Alice fumbled for a key ring, and Neveah ducked outside, ignoring the stares from a group of people huddled around the flame of a Hibachi grill. She efficiently transferred Alice's belongings to the Volkswagen, and took an extra couple of minutes to unscrew the sedan's license plates with a multi-tool from one of her pockets.

After dumping the plates and the registration papers from the glove box in with the rest of Alice's stuff, she slid behind the wheel again and put the VW in gear, heading for the nearest exit onto the freeway. Next order of business—find a hotel where no one would think to come looking for them, and then try to come up with some kind of strategy to save Alice, while also containing a mad Fae queen who could somehow cast magic despite being trapped in a human body.

Easy, she thought darkly. *What could possibly go wrong?*

TWENTY-ONE

Nigellus lay on the ground, clutching at his partially severed leg, and reflected that it had been a very long time since anyone in the three realms had truly surprised him.

Neveah — an alias chosen as a less-than-subtle joke. 'Heaven' spelled backward in Earthen English. He'd bedded the same angel whose stolen sword he'd wielded as a trophy weapon for centuries. No wonder she'd given him such an odd look the first time she'd seen him use it.

Her angelic identity didn't mean she was in any less danger now... though if she had the strength left to call the sword again, he supposed that would even the odds somewhat. It didn't change the dynamics of the underlying situation, however. Alice Ramirez could not remain on Earth while harboring the twisted soul of Queen Mab inside her.

Gritting his teeth against the pain in both his chest and his leg, he fumbled in his trouser pocket and came up with the cell phone Edward always insisted he carry. Thankfully, it hadn't been harmed during the brief battle — if such a pathetic defeat could even be called that.

Humiliation wasn't an experience with which he had much familiarity. That was yet another novelty to which the angel had introduced him, he supposed. Somehow, it was less appealing than the lust had been.

He powered on the phone, aware of how painfully slowly the healing in his leg seemed to be progressing. This entire gambit had been a tactical failure of epic proportions on his part. He thumbed the contact number for Edward's phone, and his servant picked up on the first ring.

"Sir? Were you able to find her? Where are you?"

Nigellus had to consciously unclench his jaw before he could reply. "Yes, I was able to find her, and I have no idea where I am. Please use the location tracking software on this phone and get here as fast as possible. The angel has Alice. She also has Shemasiel's blade." He forced himself to add, "And I am not currently in a condition to pursue her."

There was an uncomfortably long pause. Then, *"Neveah has your sword? Did I mishear that, sir?"*

"You did not," Nigellus bit out. "And I would appreciate your prompt arrival more than I would appreciate any commentary you might wish to offer on the matter."

"... Right," Edward replied, in the tone of one who had questions but knew better than to ask them. *"Hold for a moment and I'll get you an ETA."*

Nigellus waited while Edward pulled up the tracking app and determined his location.

"Sacramento. Blast. I'm still waiting on an Uber to get back to the house, and then it will take at least ninety minutes to drive to you." Edward hesitated. *"I might be able to get help to you more quickly than that, sir. Let me see what I can do."*

Nigellus had a good idea what that other help might entail. For the first time in his endless existence, he truly understood the human compulsion to thump one's skull against a hard surface when frustrated.

"Whatever's fastest," he said, resisting the temptation as being somehow beneath him. "Tracking the angel and Ms. Ramirez is the most pressing goal."

"*Keep your phone powered on,*" Edward said. "*I'll be as quick as I can.*"

With that, the call disconnected, leaving Nigellus to contemplate the depths of his own idiocy. He resettled his damaged leg, ignoring the flare of agony in favor of ensuring that the severed mass of muscle, bone, and ligament was positioned as close to flush as possible. He'd been a complacent fool, charging in without backup while drained to this degree. If Neveah had been alone, things might have ended very differently—but he'd also underestimated her, yet again.

A good example of an investigative reporter, indeed.

He wondered, idly, how she'd managed to find Ms. Ramirez in such a short time. With luck, he'd have a chance to ask her at some point.

Nigellus had come here with barely enough reserves to teleport himself and another person back to Vallecito. When he'd discovered that Neveah already had Alice, he'd banked everything on being able to grab the human while she was dazed and transport her directly to Hell's gate. Only inside Hell could he be certain that she was safely contained, and no longer a danger to the fragile peace.

He'd had no extra reservoir of strength for a fight... and now, he had no extra reserves left for anything. He couldn't even bloody *walk*.

That was particularly galling, since he itched to investigate the human bodies he could make out beyond the damaged chain link construction fence where he'd tried to corner the pair. There were several of them, and all quite obviously dead. That fact, coupled with Alice Ramirez' confusion and emotional upset, made him wonder.

The faintest residue of magic prickled at his skin, but he couldn't say for certain if it was the result of the angel's unexpected assault on him, or something more sinister. All he could do was lie there like a useless lump, opening himself to the trickle of ambient power as the world turned around him.

At least there appeared to be no human law enforcement response to whatever had happened, because at this point, the only thing that could heap more humiliation on his head would be the necessity of expending precious energy on influencing law enforcement to leave the scene of the crime and forget they'd seen anything.

On top of the direct physical threat—both to Neveah and any random humans who got in Mab's way—every new crime increased the chances that a police investigation would attract the attention of the Fae shadow government on Earth. Not even a demon of fate could truly see into the future, but Nigellus could picture with startling ease the sequence of events should Mab succeed in convincing other Fae of her story.

Formal renunciation of the treaty.

A new declaration of hostilities.

The siege of Hell, and the demons' inevitable response.

He could not allow any of that to happen. Not again. And yet, here he lay — waiting for his elderly human servant to arrive without benefit of any supernatural travel assistance, and meanwhile the angel gained a head start of hours.

Nigellus wanted to be angry with her. But how did one maintain anger toward an angel for the crime of trying to protect an innocent?

It wasn't as though he didn't grasp that Alice Ramirez was a blameless victim. The difference was one of practicality. Neveah seemed content to act on the vague and undefined hope that some solution could be found to exorcise Mab from the human before the Fae Queen brought war down upon all of their heads.

Nigellus... *wasn't.*

Pity he was also stuck here like a landed fish. There was no one to blame but himself. He'd jumped without thinking, out of an admittedly well-placed fear for the angel's safety. No plan, no backup, and he hadn't even told the Council about her existence here on Earth. That would come back on him soon enough, since there was no avoiding it now that Neveah had Alice.

And to think he'd called Leyak a fool for being ensorcelled by a powerful female.

He blinked up at the concrete highway deck far above him, listening to the rumble of traffic and trying to divert more healing energy to his femur, so at least the damned leg wouldn't be flopping around.

Slightly more than an hour passed before two swirls of misty vapor spiraled down to earth nearby, thickening and solidifying into a pair of familiar silhouettes in the darkness.

Zorah Bright and Ransley Thorpe stepped forward, coming to stand on either side of him. He tried not to squirm beneath their startled regard. Ransley broke the silence first, a deep furrow marring his pale brow.

"Nigellus, I hope you know I mean this in the most respectful way possible, but what the *actual fuck*?"

A muscle in Nigellus' jaw twitched.

Zorah raised a quizzical eyebrow. "Yeah, because sure—I knew intellectually about demons being able to sustain horrific injuries without dying… but I wasn't really prepared for two up-close-and-personal demonstrations in one day."

It took a concerted effort before Nigellus could spit the next words out. "I need your assistance."

"We'd gathered, after what Edward told us," Ransley said dryly. "Did Mab do this to you? And the obvious follow-up question—if she's trapped in a human body, *how* did she do this to you?"

Nigellus hesitated, weighing the possible pitfalls and benefits of revealing the whole truth. It was clear enough that Edward had convinced the pair to come to his aid, since they could fly here as mist much faster than Edward could drive. It was equally obvious that he hadn't given them any details about Neveah.

But Nigellus needed allies, and it was unlikely Neveah's secret would stay a secret much longer, regardless.

"Mab did not overpower me," he told them in a monotone. "Neveah Lane did. She escaped with Alice Ramirez, presumably intending to take her into hiding."

They both stared at him.

"Whoa. Back up a minute," Zorah said. "A tiny little human investigative reporter sliced your leg off? Dude, no offense, but the woman looks like animated singing teapots and chirping bluebirds follow her around braiding flowers in her hair all day."

Ransley raised a hand to quell her before addressing Nigellus. "You once said she was a human with natural magic. Do you still stand by that, or is there something else you're not telling us?"

So many things, Nigellus thought, with something approaching regret. *There are so many things I haven't told you.*

But in this instance, at least, it was time for the truth. "I did indeed believe that to be the case until recently. I was mistaken. Neveah Lane is the angel Shemasiel — the only member of the heavenly host still remaining on Earth."

Ransley frowned. "That's impossible."

"I assure you, it isn't," Nigellus replied tightly.

Zorah looked between them in confusion. "I thought there was no gate between Heaven and the other realms, like there is between Hell and Earth, or Earth and Dhuinne."

"There isn't," Nigellus replied. "Not anymore. The angels closed off their realm from the others when the last war started."

"And she was what? Locked out?" Ransley asked. "That seems like a bit of an oversight on someone's part."

"That is her story, yes," Nigellus said. "I have no reason to disbelieve it. As I was regrettably weakened when I arrived here, she was able to call up my blade and use it to incapacitate me so that she could escape with the possessed human."

Silence fell for a long moment.

"Holy shit," Zorah said, wide-eyed. "Okay, say what else you want to about her, but that was pretty badass."

In typical fashion, Ransley was more interested in the wider story. "Perhaps you should tell us why an angel is trying to prevent you from capturing Mab and taking her back to Hell."

Nigellus sighed. "She's attempting to save the human, Alice Ramirez. She was resistant to the idea of trapping Ms. Ramirez in Hell from the beginning—but now she has ascertained that the Council is more likely to order the human and her Fae hitchhiker executed, rather than risking Mab ever escaping again."

"Has she ascertained that *correctly*?" Zorah asked.

"Yes," Nigellus admitted.

"Then I think I'm on her side," Zorah said. "Shouldn't the goal be to get Mab out of Alice's body? That would neutralize any threat she poses, right?"

"And how do you propose to accomplish that?" Nigellus asked tiredly.

"No clue," Zorah replied without hesitation. "Not my department."

"I think we can all agree on one aspect of this, at least," Ransley said. "Having Mab-slash-Alice running around on Earth is a recipe for disaster. Can I assume she's somehow responsible for the collection of corpses over there? Or was that the angel?"

"No, that was almost certainly Mab," Nigellus told him. "In addition to the murder of Ms. Ramirez' landlady."

"Right," Ransley said. "I want to check something. Back in a tick."

He swirled away into mist and reappeared inside the construction fence, where he moved from body to body, leaning down to check each one. He reappeared at Nigellus' side a few moments later. "No obvious injuries on any of the bodies. Their positioning suggests they were blown backward by some sort of force. How's the Fae radar, luv?"

"There's something here," Zorah said. "It feels off, though."

Zorah's hybrid nature gave her a heightened sensitivity to Fae magic and its residue. That was enough to confirm Nigellus' own suspicions as to the humans' cause of death.

"*Off*, because Fae magic is somehow being filtered through a human body?" Ransley asked.

Zorah shot him an impatient look. "And how would I know that? It's magic, but it's weird. That's all I've got for you, sorry."

"We need to find her, and she already has a significant head start," Nigellus said, bringing the conversation back to the most important subject.

"If Neveah's an angel, will she be able to keep a lid on Mab?" Zorah asked. "After all, she took *you* out pretty easily, from the looks of it. Again—no offense."

"None taken." Nigellus bit the words out. "And to answer your question, the angel is severely weakened after so long without access to Heaven's power. She was shot through the heart by a booby trap left behind in Ms. Ramirez' apartment. She did not heal as one would expect an immortal to heal."

Zorah looked rather pointedly at Nigellus' leg. "Yeah, there seems to be a lot of that going around these days."

"It's healing," he said through gritted teeth.

"Perhaps we should discuss a compromise related to the current situation," Ransley said. "Firstly, do you have any way to track either Neveah or Mab directly?"

"Not anymore," Nigellus told him.

"Wonderful," the vampire said with airy sarcasm. "Can you teleport?"

"It wouldn't be prudent to attempt it at this point in time, no."

"Very well," Ransley replied. "In that case, I propose sending Zorah after your fugitive, since she has the best chance of following the trail of latent Fae magic." He shot Zorah a hard look.

"Reconnaissance only, mind you. You can trade phones with Nigellus, since his has tracking software on it."

"No arguments here," Zorah said dryly. "There's a condition, though, Nigellus. I need your word that you won't let the demons execute Alice before pursuing every possible avenue for getting Mab out of the poor girl's head."

Nigellus considered this, weighing his options. "If you agree to allow her to be taken to Hell, I will use what influence I possess to prevent her execution until all other options have been exhausted. And if Mab's soul can be successfully exorcised, I will offer the human a choice of joining the titheling village, or accepting a soul-bond so that she may leave Hell and return to Earth."

"A soul-bond with you, specifically?" Zorah pressed.

"Yes," he agreed.

She appeared to give it a moment's thought, and nodded. "Okay. Deal."

Nigellus pulled out his cell phone and proffered it. Zorah took it and gave him hers in exchange.

"The angel drives a mid-eighties white Volkswagen Rabbit with a diesel-vegetable oil conversion," Nigellus said, reflecting that this was a sentence he'd never expected to utter in the course of eternity. "Alice Ramirez reportedly owns a late model silver Ford Focus sedan. I would assume they took Neveah's car, since it can't be traced back to the human."

Zorah sighed. "Uh, baby vamp here. I have no idea what a nineteen-eighties Volkswagen Rabbit looks like, especially from above."

Ransley pulled out a phone and started typing. A moment later he turned the screen toward Zorah.

She nodded. "Oh, right. I've seen those around, I guess."

"Keep your nose peeled for the smell of popcorn or french fries coming from the exhaust," Ransley counseled, "since it's got a veggie oil conversion. Those are fairly rare, even in California."

"Well, I mean, I'll be flying around as mist," Zorah pointed out. "But I'll do my best. You two aren't going to try to kill each other if I leave you alone, right?"

"He's immortal, and I'm a rare source of vampire blood that he desperately needs to keep safe," Ransley pointed out. "Go on, luv. Get a shift on. Nigellus and I will stay here and have a nice little chat while we're waiting for Edward to show up with a car."

He smiled, showing fang, and Nigellus swallowed another sigh.

TWENTY-TWO

This had, Nigellus supposed, been a long time coming. "I don't suppose you'd care to make another blood donation while we're waiting?" he said, once Zorah had transformed into mist and swirled away.

Ransley crouched next to him, elbows propped loosely on knees. "No," he said. "Considering how much I've already bled for demons today, I don't suppose I would."

"You obviously have things you wish to say to me," Nigellus told him. "You might as well go ahead and say them."

"You know," Ransley said after a short pause, "I find it fascinating how hard you're willing to fight for people, despite seeming to regard them as little more than pawns on a chessboard most of the time."

"Odd," Nigellus said in a monotone. "You're the second person to accuse me of that in slightly more than an hour."

"Hmm. Imagine that." Ransley tilted his head. "So, the Council really had no idea that they were holding the Fae queen prisoner for all those years?"

"I should think the Council's reaction to Leyak's revelation speaks for itself," Nigellus said.

The vampire appeared to weigh that for a moment. "Yes, I suppose it does." Silence stretched. "If there's about to be another war, don't expect me to become your foot soldier again, Nigellus. I won't fight for you. I won't allow Zorah to fight for you. And I think I can safely say that Guthrie Leonides will tell you to go fuck yourself if you try to press-gang him into fighting your battles."

Pain that had nothing to do with his injured heart speared through Nigellus' chest. Ransley and Zorah had already contributed to the demons' future martial strategy via the medium of their blood. Should the Fae declare war again, he wasn't fool enough to think he could shelter the three remaining vampires from what would come next.

"Let us hope it doesn't come to that," was all he said.

Ransley nodded. "Well, that's certainly a text-book demon non-answer if I've ever heard one. Witness my surprise."

Nigellus didn't rise to the barb.

"You know," the vampire continued, "I can actually hear the things you don't want to say aloud." He settled into a seated position on the ground. "If the demons decide they need us, they can always simply take control of our will and force us to turn other vampires for a new army, whether we want to or not."

It was a painfully accurate assessment, and Nigellus covered a wince.

"You think that by turning the human tithel-ings you've been stockpiling in Hell into vampires, you can raise a new undead fighting force with resistance to the Fae weapon that killed my people last time," Ransley went on inexorably. "Raise them up on diluted vampire blood to make them stronger and extend their life spans, then hope that their previous exposure to Dhuinne means they won't immediately become cannon fodder, right? Well, I have news for you, Nigellus. Just because the Fae kidnapped them from Earth as infants and held them in Dhuinne for a few months doesn't mean they're somehow inoculated against Fae magic."

This, apparently, was the heart of Ransley's current grudge against him—not, as he'd originally thought, bitterness over Nigellus having saved him and then wiped his memories.

Interesting.

"In addition to being the second person to accuse me of treating sentient beings as chess pieces, you are also the second person to surprise me today, Ransley," he said. "But I ask you this. Would you truly prefer Hell to step back and allow the Fae to run roughshod across three realms?"

The vampire's expression closed off. "Two realms, surely. We both know that the Fae won't invade Hell—not when doing so would only make them prisoners inside it. Which brings me neatly to my point. If this doomsday scenario occurs, and the Council votes to force the birth of more vampires… give me your word that you will keep Zorah safe inside Hell as long as there's danger for her outside it."

Nigellus met his former protégé's startling blue eyes and held them. "*Ransley.* Should the worst occur, I will do that much for both of you. Was there really a question?"

Ransley pinched the bridge of his nose and let out a pained breath of laughter. "Yes, Nigellus. There really was." He looked up and shook his head ruefully. "I feel as though I should also be bargaining for Guthrie while I've got you in such an accommodating mood, but we both know he'd spit in your face if you suggested he run away and hide in Hell."

"I'm sure he would," Nigellus agreed.

Ransley turned away, speaking under his breath. "God, I hate all of this so much." Then, in a more normal tone, "Right. Let's get you patched up enough so that you can at least stand by the time Edward arrives."

"I thought you'd already bled enough for demons today," Nigellus observed, as Ransley leaned over him and opened a vein.

"I lied." Blood dripped over the gaping wound, bringing a fresh wash of healing power. "But try not to do anything in the next little while that will make me regret it."

If only life were that simple.

"Thank you," Nigellus told him, rather than make any promises he might not be able to keep.

"I'll have to feed soon if I'm going to be any use at all for whatever comes next," Ransley warned. "And you need to start scoping out other potential allies, in case Zorah isn't able to find Mab. Frankly, I doubt we're going to be able to tie up this mess with a neat bow. Have you considered the cat-sidhe?"

"They are already apprised of the situation, though not of the escaped prisoner's identity." Nigellus cautiously released his grip on his leg. It stayed attached, which was forward progress of a sort.

"Good," Ransley said. "What about Albigard? He might be Unseelie, but he's never been a fan of Dhuinne's warmongering. Plus, there's the small fact that Mab sacrificed his brother and sister's lives to power the Vampire Killer. He's more likely to try and stick a sword through her himself than to run crying to the Fae Court about it."

That was admittedly not an angle Nigellus had considered. "I'd hoped to prevent information about this incident reaching any more people than absolutely necessary, but your point is well taken. It may come to that, if we're not able to track down Neveah and her fugitive promptly."

"Yes, *Neveah*," Ransley said, retaking his seat next to Nigellus. "Perhaps you'd like to share that story while we're waiting—because you were awfully quick to charge back to Earth with a half-baked plan when you thought she might be in danger." He frowned. "I mean—an angel, Nigellus, *really*? Do I have to be the one to point out what a terrible cliché that is?"

Nigellus lay back and closed his eyes. "Would you please allow me to keep the pathetic modicum of dignity I still have remaining, Ransley?"

"I'll get the story eventually, you know," said the vampire. "But keep your secrets if you must." He gave a rueful snort. "I suppose I don't have a leg to stand on, given the circumstances of my first meeting with Zorah."

That had, by all accounts, been a less than auspicious introduction—but Nigellus raised his head and eyed Ransley narrowly. "'A leg to stand on'? Was that *truly* necessary?"

Ransley raised a dark eyebrow, unrepentant. "You're the one worried about dignity. Don't worry—Edward should be here before too much longer. I've seen the way that man drives."

"And yet, he's never damaged the paint job on a two-hundred-thousand dollar Aston Martin by getting into a car chase," Nigellus murmured, lying back again.

Ransley wisely didn't reply. They waited in silence for Edward's arrival. Nigellus was surprised to find that it wasn't an uncomfortable silence.

TWENTY-THREE

"Wait, I need to go north!" Alice cried, peering at the signage as they passed an intersection.

Neveah had taken Highway 84 south out of Sacramento, heading toward Rio Vista. She had no illusions regarding the kinds of resources that Nigellus and the Demon Council were likely to throw at discovering her whereabouts. Not now that they knew the identity of Alice's hitchhiker—and knew that Neveah was attempting to protect her.

"Don't worry," she told her passenger. "That's where we're ultimately going. We're just taking a bit of a detour first to make sure no one's following us."

Neveah still had her phone with her, and the trick she'd used to find Alice had given her an idea. It seemed plausible that Nigellus would make the same logical leaps she had, and theorize that Mab would be heading for the nearest concentration of Fae that she knew about, in what was now Seattle. Given that fact, she'd bet money that Nigellus would assume Neveah was trying to prevent Mab from going there.

So, first Neveah would drive south for a bit. Then she would hide her cell phone in a convenience store where the employees wouldn't be likely to stumble across it for a while. And finally, she would circle around to head north after all. If they tracked her phone, they'd find exactly what they expected to find—a southerly route.

The thing was, Mab could find Fae pretty much anywhere in the country if she only knew to look. There was no additional risk in heading the direction she wanted to head, and it might help to keep her docile.

That was the big question right now. Neveah had a theory regarding Mab's lack of appearance since the incident at the construction site, but there was no way to test it at present. No *direct* way, at any rate.

"What's up north?" she asked casually. "Where are you headed?"

She chanced a sideways glance at the human. Alice opened her mouth as though to answer, only to close it again and frown.

"I… uh… it's just…" Another pause. "There are some people I need to see. In… that place with the big bay. You know?"

"Seattle?" Neveah asked.

Alice's expression cleared. "Yes, that's the one."

"Then that's where we'll head," she replied easily. "It's a long way, though. You know that, right? We should stop somewhere along the way to rest overnight."

Alice hesitated before giving a slow nod. "Okay. I *am* really tired."

"Great," Neveah told her. "I need to make a stop in Rio Vista, and then we'll get turned around and head up the coast until we find a good place to stop for the night. Are you hungry?"

"Starving," Alice said.

Neveah didn't doubt it, after her human body had acted as a conduit for enough Fae magic to kill five people in an instant. And that was yet another concern. Some humans possessed a hint of natural magic — the legacy of limited interbreeding with Fae in the distant past. But they were in no way designed to channel the kind of power that Mab was somehow pouring through Alice.

Neveah didn't know what the repercussions of that were likely to be, or how soon they were likely to manifest. She would wager it was the magical expenditure that had weakened Mab's hold and allowed Alice's consciousness to come to the fore, though. Neveah was banking on Mab being out for a few hours, at least.

She'd been unprepared for the Fae to still have usable magic. She needed to *get* prepared, and fast — but it would all be moot if Nigellus caught up to them first. So — convenience store, motel room, and she would deal with the other part once those things were taken care of.

In Rio Vista, she headed west on Highway 12 and pulled into a truck stop. As much as it irked her, she filled the Rabbit up with diesel, since this was definitely not the time to go begging for used cooking grease at the McDonald's down the street. Inside the store, she locked her phone screen and slid it beneath a set of metal shelves holding automotive supplies while no one was looking.

She replaced it with a thirty-dollar burner phone from behind the checkout counter, since she would still need to begin the convoluted process of contacting the cat-sidhe. That process began with a call to a human from one of the old families in County Meath, Ireland who still served the Fae openly. Exiting with the new phone, a selection of snack food, and a box of Sominex, she returned to find Alice huddled in the passenger seat, half asleep.

"Food," she said, handing Alice a bag of trail mix and a bottle of cranberry cocktail. "Oh, and take two of these. You look like you've got one hell of a headache."

She handed over a couple of the sleeping pills, and Alice swallowed them without asking what they were.

"Good girl," Neveah told her. "We're going to swing around and head north along the coast now. Once we've got a bit more distance between us and Sacramento, I'll find us someplace to crash for the night."

"'Kay," Alice said in a tiny voice. "I still need to call my parents, too."

"In the morning," Neveah said firmly, knowing she'd need to come up with some better excuse for why that was a bad idea by then. "For now, eat. And if you want to doze, go right ahead. You must be completely exhausted."

Alice shivered, but focused her attention on the trail mix rather than answering. Half an hour later, she was fast asleep, snoring lightly and drooling on Neveah's passenger side window.

Neveah drove west to Petaluma and found a questionable looking Motel 8 that accepted cash. The place was practically empty, which suited her just fine. She chivvied a groggy Alice into the ground-floor room, where the human promptly faceplanted on the nearest of the two beds and started snoring again.

Neveah brought Alice's belongings inside and took the chance to do a thorough search. It was what you'd expect for a human on the run — basic clothing, toiletries, and cash. No sign of a bloody heart packed in salt, which was reassuring in some ways and concerning in others. Either Alice had ditched Leyak's heart, or she'd gone to the effort of stashing it somewhere when she'd fled her apartment. As long as it was still in salt, neither option did Leyak much good, but Neveah was hoping for the first one on general principals.

The drive here had given her time to ponder the horrific scar on Nigellus' chest, combined with his weakened state. She knew she shouldn't have been able to gain the upper hand against him as easily as she had. There was only one reason she could think of why his chest might have been cut open shortly before he discovered the identity of Hell's escaped prisoner.

Leyak lacked his heart, and that had kept him from telling what he knew about Mab's escape. Apparently, Nigellus had lent him one long enough to get the information he'd needed. It was just possible that Neveah had underestimated the lengths to which the demon would go in pursuit of the Council's goals.

She repacked all of Alice's belongings exactly as she'd found them, confident that there were no hidden weapons or anything else dangerous. Then, she put in the first call that would eventually connect her to the cat-sidhe, after which she settled in to wait… and to think. She had the broad outlines of a plan to contain Mab, though she would need a few supplies first. The issue was the risk involved in leaving Alice alone for any length of time — hence the current experiment with the sleeping pills.

They seemed to be working, but since Mab had already been absent from Alice's consciousness after the explosion of magic, she wanted to give it a few more hours to be sure. If Mab could be rendered harmless with drugs that affected her stolen human body, Neveah could work with that until she was able to meet in person with the cat-sidhe. It still wasn't great for Alice's health, but it was far preferable to the alternative.

The minutes ticked by, lengthening into hours as Neveah stood silent sentry. In her life as Shemasiel, she had been a Watcher. That background held her in good stead now.

The red numbers on the cheap digital alarm clock next to the bed read three-twenty a.m. when Alice whimpered and began to twitch, apparently in the throes of a nightmare. Neveah swung her legs off the mattress of the second bed and turned on one of the lamps. While she didn't need the light to see, she suspected Alice wouldn't appreciate waking to pitch darkness in an unfamiliar room.

The human whimpered, mumbling things like, "*No, stop,*" and "*please, you can't.*" Abruptly, she flailed, coming awake with a cry. Neveah took note that it was roughly the time when the sleeping pills might have been expected to wear off normally.

"Alice," she said, in her best reassuring tone. "Easy now. You're safe. You just had a nightmare." She settled on the edge of the human's bed and put a hand on her shoulder. It was shuddering, and her breath came in great, rasping gulps.

"It wasn't a nightmare," Alice said. "Oh my god—I... I remember! Mrs. Fitzwilliams, she's—" The words cut off in a choked sob, and the human descended into wracking tears.

Neveah was willing to bet that Mrs. Fitzwilliams had been the landlady.

"I didn't want to do it!" Alice sobbed. "That wasn't me—I couldn't have done that! *How could I have done that?*"

Neveah's instincts reared up. Protect. Nurture. Avenge, when necessary. She took Alice's shoulders in her hands, squeezing until the human lifted crying, bloodshot eyes to meet hers.

"Listen to me, Alice," she said. "Those terrible things were *not* your fault. Something else is controlling you—something foul and angry and bitter. I'm going to find a way to get it out of you. And until then, I *will* keep you safe... I swear it."

Alice had listened wide-eyed, not looking away despite her hitching sobs. But now, her demeanor changed. Her shoulders straightened beneath Neveah's grip, and her expression went still and cold. Neveah stared into eyes that kindled with a spark of glowing green, like the forest on a sunlit day. A slow, twisted smile pulled at Alice's pale lips.

"How sweet," said the thing that wasn't Alice. "And tell me, little creature—who will keep *you* safe… *from me?*"

Neveah let the human's shoulders go and stood up slowly from the edge of the bed. Righteous anger flared in her chest as she contemplated this being who would steal a stranger's life, simply because of her own bitter selfishness to survive at any cost.

The demons held moral culpability for their willingness to punish an innocent human. But *here* was where the true guilt lay—in this cold, heartless Fae who murdered and tormented without conscience. Neveah took a step back, then another, and another, putting space between them. Without taking her eyes off the Seelie Queen, she reached inward, assessing what strength she still had. Her flaming sword floated in the pocket dimension where she'd hidden it. Her wings fluttered, tucked away in their liminal space.

Neveah narrowed her eyes. "Oh, so you want another victim, do you? You want an excuse to fling some more magic around?"

She lifted her right hand, fingers ready and waiting to close around her weapon's familiar hilt in preparation for enacting the next part of her plan.

"Go ahead, then," she taunted. "*Bring it, bitch.*"

End of Book One

Nigellus and Neveah's story continues in *The Sixth Demon: Book Two.*

To discover more books by this author, visit www.rasteffan.com